CAUGHT!

Under his weight the foot Ki had planted so carefully broke through the crusted sandy soil. Ki fought to keep his balance.

Mole was the first of the outlaws to turn when the grating of Ki's feet broke the almost total silence. Ki saw Mole bringing up his pistol and tried to throw his body to one side but his awkward posture defeated him. He did not hear the report of Mole's shot, for speeding with the report the pistol-slug struck Ki at the roots of his thick black hair. Its impact cut a shallow groove in his scalp as it plowed through his hair and whistled past him, and his consciousness went.

Ki was toppling forward when Mole fired his second round. . . .

Also in the LONE STAR series
from Jove

LONGARM AND THE LONE STAR LEGEND
LONE STAR ON THE TREACHERY TRAIL
LONE STAR AND THE OPIUM RUSTLERS
LONE STAR AND THE BORDER BANDITS
LONE STAR AND THE KANSAS WOLVES
LONE STAR AND THE CALIFORNIA OIL WAR
LONE STAR AND THE ALASKAN GUNS
LONE STAR AND THE WHITE RIVER CURSE
LONE STAR AND THE TOMBSTONE GAMBLE
LONE STAR AND THE TIMBERLAND TERROR
LONE STAR IN THE CHEROKEE STRIP
LONE STAR AND THE OREGON RAIL SABOTAGE
LONE STAR AND THE MISSION WAR
LONE STAR AND THE GUNPOWDER CURE
LONE STAR AND THE LAND BARONS
LONE STAR AND THE GULF PIRATES
LONE STAR AND THE INDIAN REBELLION
LONE STAR AND THE NEVADA MUSTANGS
LONE STAR AND THE CON MAN'S RANSOM
LONE STAR AND THE STAGE COACH WAR
LONE STAR AND THE TWO GUN KID
LONE STAR AND THE SIERRA SWINDLERS
LONE STAR IN THE BIG HORN MOUNTAINS
LONE STAR AND THE DEATH TRAIN
LONE STAR AND THE RUSTLER'S AMBUSH
LONE STAR AND THE TONG'S REVENGE
LONE STAR AND THE OUTLAW POSSE
LONE STAR AND THE SKY WARRIORS
LONE STAR IN A RANGE WAR
LONE STAR AND THE PHANTOM GUNMEN
LONE STAR AND THE MONTANA LAND GRAB
LONE STAR AND THE JAMES GANG'S LOOT
LONE STAR AND THE MASTER OF DEATH
LONE STAR AND THE CHEYENNE TRACKDOWN
LONE STAR AND THE LOST GOLD MINE
LONE STAR AND THE COMANCHEROS
LONE STAR AND HICKOK'S GHOST
LONE STAR AND THE DEADLY STRANGER
LONE STAR AND THE SILVER BANDITS
LONE STAR AND THE NEVADA BLOODBATH
LONE STAR IN THE BIG THICKET
LONE STAR AND THE SUICIDE SPREAD
LONE STAR AND THE TEXAS RANGERS
LONE STAR AND THE DEATH MERCHANTS
LONE STAR IN A COMSTOCK CROSSFIRE
LONE STAR AND THE MEDICINE LODGE SHOOT-OUT
LONE STAR AND THE BARBARY KILLERS
LONE STAR AND THE ROGUE GRIZZLIES
LONE STAR IN HELL'S CANYON
LONE STAR ON THE WARPATH
LONE STAR AND THE DIAMOND SWINDLERS

WESLEY ELLIS

LONE STAR AND THE DIAMOND SWINDLERS

JOVE BOOKS, NEW YORK

LONE STAR AND THE DIAMOND SWINDLERS

A Jove Book / published by arrangement with
the author

PRINTING HISTORY
Jove edition / September 1989

ISBN: 0-515-10131-1

Jove Books are published by The Berkley Publishing Group,
200 Madison Avenue, New York, New York 10016.

PRINTED IN THE UNITED STATES OF AMERICA

10 9 8 7 6 5 4 3 2 1

★

Chapter 1

"I've never been as glad that I missed an appointment as I am about the one that got mixed up in San Francisco, Jessie," Harmon Marsden said. "If I hadn't gone back to the hotel when I did, I wouldn't've run into you."

"You know that I'm not exactly unhappy myself about us running into each other," said Jessie, smiling. "This has been one of the most pleasant trips I've ever made going back to the Circle Star."

Jessie and Marsden were leaning back on their pillows in the bed that dominated the master stateroom of Marsden's luxurious private railroad car. A chill-beaded bottle of dry white wine stood on the small table at Marsden's elbow. The frosted shade of the ceiling lamp was swaying gently in rhythm with the *click-clack* of the car's wheels on the tracks as the Limited sped over the rails on its eastward schedule.

Except for the half-day layover in the small but growing town of Los Angeles, while they waited for the private car to be switched and coupled to the east-bound Limited, Jessie and her lover had seldom been out of the stateroom since leaving San Francisco. They'd encountered each other by accident in the lobby of the St. Francis Hotel while both were checking out.

"Jessie!" Marsden had exclaimed. "I didn't even know you were here in San Francisco! How could we have missed meeting before, both of us being here in the same hotel?"

"Probably because Ki and I didn't check in until last night." Jessie had smiled. "We're just getting back from the trip I try to make at least once a year to check on the properties I have here on the coast."

"And you're leaving now to go back to your ranch?"

"Of course. I'm running a bit late, and I'll miss part of the fall roundup, but I'll be back at the Circle Star in time for the gathers and to look over the market herd before it's shipped."

Marsden had hesitated for a thoughtful moment before he replied, then he'd said, "I don't suppose it'd make any difference to your plans if you got back to Texas a few hours later than you'd intended to?"

"And stay here in San Francisco so that we can spend the evening together?"

"Not exactly. I'll have to go by the schedule I've already set up, Jessie. I'm sure you understand why."

"Of course, Harmon. Your office probably has appointments scheduled right now for the first few days after you get back."

Marsden smiled. His grin was infectious. It made his face seem younger and less sober, and was one of the features that had attracted Jessie to him at their first meeting several years earlier.

"I'm due at the depot in another hour, and it'll take almost half an hour to get there. It's a long way, Jessie."

"I was just about to tell you, Harmon. I can't change my schedule any more than you can shift yours around."

"What I really started to say," Marsden went on, "was that it seems to me you and Ki might enjoy making the trip back to Texas with me in my private car. You'll only be a few hours later getting back than you would be if you took the Express."

Jessie was silent for a moment, then her thoughtful frown was banished by a smile. She said, "Well, when you put it that way—"

Marsden broke in, "Being with you again even for the few days we'd have together traveling to Texas would go a long way toward making up for the months we've been apart."

"It has been a long time," said Jessie, nodding. A smile that matched Marsden's stole over her face as she went on: "And the little difference in the time spent getting back isn't all that important. Yes, Harmon. I can send a telegram to the stationmaster at our little whistle-stop, and he'll see that it's delivered to my foreman at the ranch. I'll enjoy being with you instead of the two of us just saying hello and good-bye here in the St. Francis lobby."

During the long trip back to Texas, Jessie and Marsden had spent most of their time in his stateroom. Ki and Marsden's valet picked up their off-and-on rivalry over the chessboard. Their competition was one of long standing, going back to the time several years before when Jessie and Marsden had first become lovers.

Aside from mealtimes, the lovers had been alone, and they recaptured as much as possible of the time they'd been separated. Marsden was kept in New York most of the time by family business matters which he'd inherited from his father, and Jessie was kept in Texas by the responsibilities that had come to her due to Alex Starbuck's untimely death. Now, with only an hour or so before the train would reach the little whistle-stop station that served the sprawling Circle Star, Jessie turned to her lover.

"Are you sure you've got to go on?" she asked. "Even though I know you're busy, I'd love to have you stay at the Circle Star for a few days. It's been a long time since you've been there."

"I'd like nothing better, Jessie," Marsden told her. "But as I told you in San Francisco, I've got to get back to New York, just as you've got to get back to your ranch."

"Then we'd better make the most of the time we have left."

Jessie set her wineglass aside and turned to her lover. Marsden found her waiting lips, and while they held their kiss, his hands caressed Jessie's full budded breasts.

Although she and Marsden had been together almost without interruption since leaving San Francisco, Jessie had seen no one during her long trip who'd appealed to her as a bed partner. The wise old geisha to whom Alex Starbuck had entrusted Jessie's sexual education had cautioned her about the danger that could follow an affair with an employee, and Jessie had never fallen into the trap of an involvement with one of the hands. Now, on her way back to the Circle Star for what could be a long period of isolation, she was ready to go more than halfway in matching Marsden's caresses.

Almost breathless after their prolonged embrace, she broke their kiss and began stroking her lover's body, her hands as light as the wings of a butterfly and her lips even softer and much warmer as she moved them, following the path of her hand caresses down his ribs and hips.

Marsden was already half-erect after their prolonged kiss, and when he felt Jessie's soft lips engulfing him, he lay back and closed his eyes while she made full use of the lessons she'd been taught by her geisha mentor. Then, when her lover had fully recovered, he began lavishing on Jessie his version of the caresses that he'd received. She closed her eyes and accepted the soft luxury of Marsden's ardent attentions until the storm of fulfillment swept over her and passed and they lay side by side in a gentle embrace while passions ebbed and were renewed.

Marsden went into her then, and soon Jessie was gasping and bringing up her hips with a mounting flurry of desire that matched his lusty thrusts. They prolonged their embrace until their climax could no longer be denied. Still joined, they tossed and sighed and kissed as their final moments peaked and passed, then lay quietly side by side as the train chugged across the rolling Texas prairie.

They slept briefly, entwined in close embrace, until the faint shrieking of the engine's whistle warned them that their journey together was nearing its end.

"Why don't you change your mind about getting off at the Circle Star stop, Jessie?" Marsden asked as he stepped into his shoes and began buttoning them.

"I can't because I've got to be at the ranch when the hands are shaping up the market herd. My foreman's a good man, but I want to pass on every steer in a Circle Star herd that's going to market."

"I can understand that," Marsden said, nodding. "But it'd only mean an extra day if you went on to San Antonio, or two days if you went as far as Fort Worth."

"And another day spent getting back from San Antonio or two more spent coming back from Fort Worth," Jessie reminded him. "But even one extra day just isn't in the cards."

"Surely a day or two more before you get to your ranch won't matter all that much!" Marsden protested.

"When the market herd's being loaded is the one time of year when I feel like I really have to be at the Circle Star," Jessie explained. "I'm not going to have my ranch's reputation hurt by shipping a raunched steer to market."

"I'm afraid you're talking outside of my vocabulary," he said, smiling. "Just what do you mean by a 'raunched' steer?'

"A steer that's sick or acts like it's about to be. Or one that's been in a fight and gotten gored, anything that cuts down its market value," she explained. "I've got a good foreman, and I don't usually have to second-guess him, but the Circle Star's my ranch and the market herd's my responsibility."

"You're Alex's daughter, all right," Marsden said with a smile. "He always was a stickler for things like that. I've heard my own father say that too many times ever to forget it."

"Alex was a good teacher," Jessie went on. "And I'll bet that right now there's a line of cattle cars standing on the railroad siding, waiting to be loaded."

"And you feel like you have to be there to watch."

"Of course I do!" Then Jessie's voice softened, but not with the softness of surrender to his plea, as she went on: "I'd be as lost without the Circle Star as you'd be if you didn't have your offices and banks and the New York Stock Exchange to hold your interest."

Marsden nodded. "I suppose I understand. But perhaps you'll find time to visit me in the East, after your market herd's been shipped. Won't things be fairly dull on your ranch then?"

"Things are never dull on a spread as big as the Circle Star," Jessie said with a smile. "But I haven't visited in the East for quite some time. Perhaps I will make a trip to your town a little later in the summer. I'll see how things shape up and let you know."

"Well, Miss Jessie, far as I can tell, we'll be able to finish cutting out the market steers before tomorrow's over," Ed Wright, the Circle Star foreman, told Jessie. It was early evening, Jessie's first full day at the ranch after her arrival the previous day, and he'd come to give Jessie a report on the progress of shaping up the market herd for shipping. "I guess you'll want to start driving the critters to the railroad spur the day after?"

"Do you think the men will need a day to rest before we start the drive, Ed?" Jessie asked.

"There ain't none of 'em that'd balk at a day off about this time, after all the riding they been doing, cutting out," Ed said. "But they're ready to start moving if you say the word."

"Then let's finish the job now," Jessie replied. "We'll start for the railroad tomorrow, get the steers loaded and on their way. You can tell the men they'll get their day off when we get back."

"Whatever you say," Ed said. "I guess you'll be riding with us, like always?"

"I wouldn't miss it for the world," Jessie said, smiling. "Ki and I will be with you and the men at daybreak, and we'll stay with you until the last critter goes up the loading chute."

"There are only two more cars to load," Ki told Jessie as he reined in beside her. "And that bunch that Ed and the men are chousing along the tracks will fill them. If they work fast we can get them in the car before dark."

"Ed and Shorty are all packed and ready to go with them, I hope."

"From what they were saying a little while ago, they're planning a high old time in Fort Worth before they start back."

"They're entitled to it, I'm sure." Jessie smiled.

"You can see," Ki told her. "They're getting ready now to load the last two cars."

He gestured toward the railroad siding where the slat-sided cattle cars were resting. Beside the track of the railroad spur, between it and the main line, three or four Circle Star hands were driving a loose gaggling line of steers toward the end of the string of waiting cattle cars.

"I've been watching," Jessie replied. "And keeping tally. We're going to wind up with three extra steers."

"Then we'll have to put twenty-five in each of those last two cars and find another car where we can squeeze in the other extra."

"I'm sure Ed's already got that worked out, Ki. We don't have to—" She stopped short when the distant wailing of a train whistle made itself heard above the blatting of the cattle and the shouts of the hands, then went on: "That must be the engine that's coming to haul our cars, Ki. And it's right on time. We ought to have our cars ready by the time it gets here."

"We will have," Ki assured her. "It'll take the train crew a little while to throw switches and couple up, but our steers should be moving to market in less than an hour."

They stood watching the activity as the Circle Star hands joined in prodding—and sometimes pushing—

the steers into the first of the two remaining cattle cars. The sounds of the engine that was approaching grew steadily louder, then came into view. Jessie studied it for a moment, and a frown formed on her face.

"That's not our engine, Ki!" she said. "It's a train! And moving fast. I hope the men by the tracks get the cattle in those cars before it gets here!"

"Yes, they're all fresh from the range and might spook," Ki said. "The last thing we need right now is to have a train pull in. But you said the stationmaster—"

"He did!" Jessie broke in to explain. "But if you remember, he's substituting for the regular stationman for a while. I took special pains to tell him that we had to have a loading time when there wouldn't be any trains due to pass on the main line, but I guess he didn't understand that train whistles frighten range-raised cattle and start them running."

Ki was already reining his horse around. Jessie touched Sun's flank with the toe of her boot, and the magnificent palomino also started moving. Even before they'd moved, it was too late. The whistle of the approaching train sounded again, this time louder. Jessie and Ki could see the engine now, and in a moment they also saw the fresh bursts of steam from its whistle as the engineer loosed the series of short toots which were the signal to the stationmaster that the train had almost reached its stopping point.

When the cattle between the tracks heard the closer whistle blast, its noise completed the spooking that the first wails had begun. The half-hundred head of steers broke their line and in little groups of three or four or a half-dozen headed away from the right-of-way and spilled out straggling onto the open prairie beyond the tracks in spite of the efforts of the cowhands to bunch them.

Jessie and Ki got there in time to help, and the men who'd clustered beside the depot after finishing their jobs swung back into their saddles at once to lend a hand. The oncoming train had come into sight by now, and once more its whistle sounded. The strange new noise even closer at hand and the sight of the locomotive with its spouting stack as well as the sound of its drivers and the rumbling of the cars it was pulling only made the scattered cattle run even more wildly.

Two or three of the horses, accustomed only to the silent ranges of the big Circle Star, were also spooked by the locomotive. They began to buck and leap, forcing the men mounted on them to abandon their efforts to help while they calmed their feisty mounts.

In spite of the few minutes of confusion when the steers first broke, most of the Circle Star hands were veterans at their jobs. They fanned out, headed beyond the running steers, then turned their horses and began chousing them back into an orderly herd once more.

Jessie could see very quickly that the hands had the situation under control. She reined Sun around and galloped back to the depot, where the train had stopped. Sun was not a range horse. The big palomino was accustomed to strange sights and sounds and was also too well-trained to panic. In addition, there was the mystic bond which so often forms between horse and human, and which seems to allow some horses almost to anticipate the wishes of their rider. This was the kind of bond which existed to a very strong degree between Sun and Jessie.

Sun knew that as long as Jessie was on his back, the world was all right. He made no false moves when she guided him at his fastest gait beside the locomotive just as it started to pull away from the little depot. Jessie waved to the engineer, trying to signal him to stop, but he mistook the wave for a friendly greeting and waved back. Then with a final whistle toot the engineer opened the throttle, and the train began gathering speed. At that point Jessie reined in. She sat for a moment in angry frustration watching the train, then touched the reins to turn Sun around and rode back to rejoin her ranch hands.

They had the incipient stampede under control by now and were bunching the steers to return them to the cattle car. Ki saw Jessie approaching and rode to meet her.

"I thought for a minute we might be in trouble," he said. "But the men did a good job of heading off those free steers, and a fast one as well."

"They certainly did," Jessie agreed as she glanced along the rails at the little knot of steers now being driven back to the cattle cars by the Circle Star hands. "I think we'll be better off letting them finish the loading job instead of trying to help them. Besides, I want to have a word with that stationmaster."

"I'll go along, if you don't object, Jessie. I'd like to hear what he has to say."

They covered the short distance to the station in silence, reined in, and went inside. The stationmaster was sitting at his worktable behind a counter that spanned the small room.

"I thought you told me that there wouldn't be any trains passing while we were loading our Circle Star cattle," Jessie said. Her voice showed no anger. "I suppose you saw what happened when that train whistled a while ago."

"There wasn't supposed to be," the man replied. The tone of his voice indicated that he was ready to defend his job as well as his employer. "Thing is, that train was due to go past here last night, but a couple of cars got derailed back to the east, someplace just this side of Uvalde. It's throwed my whole da— my whole schedule outa kilter, Miss Starbuck. Trouble is, the dispatcher back there in Uvalde never did get on the wire like he should've and told me it'd be passing, but I figured you'd have all your stock loaded by the time it passed here."

"What about the locomotive that's supposed to be here to get our cattle shipment moving as soon as the cars are loaded?" she asked. "Is it going to be delayed by the derailment?"

"Not as far as I know," the stationmaster replied. "It oughta be here any minute now. If it ain't, I'll get on the wire to Uvalde and see what the dispatcher says about it."

"And you'll let me know at once, I—" Jessie broke off as another wailing engine whistle sounded in the distance. "Perhaps you won't need to worry," she went on. "I hope that's the engine whistling now."

★

Chapter 2

Jessie stepped out onto the station platform. A locomotive with only its tender and a caboose behind it was within a few hundred feet of the depot and was closing the gap fast. It was obviously the engine that had been sent to pull the loaded cattle cars to Fort Worth, and Jessie could not hold back a sigh of relief.

She glanced along the tracks at the loaded cattle cars and saw that the hands had not only managed to get the bunch of bolted steers back to the cars but were already beginning to load them. A quick mental tally of the animals still waiting on the right-of-way told her that the Circle Star wranglers had already loaded more than half of the bolted bunch.

Even at a distance Jessie could see that Ki and Ed Wright were working just as hard as the others as they tried to get their job finished before the approaching engine slowed to a halt beside the long string of cattle cars.

"Miss Jessica Starbuck?" a man's voice coming from behind her broke into Jessie's watching.

"Yes," she replied, turning to face the speaker. She saw not one man, but two.

"My name's Jack Johnson," the man went on. "And this is Tek Powell. We've come all the way from California to talk to you. We'd've been here sooner, but nobody told us this is just a whistle-stop. We went on past it to the next town and then had to come all the way back, and—"

"I don't mean to seem rude or impatient, Mr. Johnson," Jessie broke in when the newcomer showed no signs of slackening his flow of words. "But I'm trying to get a herd of cattle off to the livestock yards in Fort Worth, and I don't really have time to chat with you right now."

"Why, I can understand that, if it's your cows on that train standing back yonder," Johnson said. "You just go on about your business. Tek and me don't mind waiting. We'll just stand right here until you're through."

Jessie realized that in the isolation of the whistle-stop there'd be no reasonable way to avoid listening to whatever get-rich-quick proposition the stranger intended to offer her. She made the best of her situation and smiled as she said, "That'll be fine. I'll have a few minutes to listen to you as soon as my cattle move out. Now, if you'll excuse me, I'm going to ride down to where they're loading those cars and make sure that everything's in good shape."

Without waiting for a reply, Jessie stepped off the depot platform and levered herself into Sun's saddle. She let the big palomino pick its own path along the right-of-way until she got to the end of the string of cattle cars. Dismounting, she picked her way across the tracks to the end of the last car, where Ki was standing talking with Ed Wright. They broke off their conversation when they saw her coming to join them and waited until she reached them.

"Ed and I were just talking about unloading at the stockyards and what he and Shorty were to do before they start back," Ki volunteered.

"You've been through the stockyards routine enough times to know what they'll have to take care of as well as I do, Ki," Jessie said. "Maybe even better. As long as they remember about the waybills and the auctioneer's receipts and the other little bits of red tape, I'm sure they won't have any trouble."

"I don't imagine we'll have none, Miss Jessie," Wright broke in. "And don't worry about me and Shorty behaving right. We know you ain't sending us all the way to Fort Worth just to look for the elephant and listen for the owl-hoot. That ain't to say we won't step up to the bar a time or two, but we'll be back prompt-like and in good shape."

"I'm not a bit worried, Ed." Jessie smiled. "I want you to enjoy your trip as long as the Circle Star business isn't neglected. We'll expect you back in about two weeks. But now if you'll just take charge here and get these cattle cars started moving, there are a few things I need to discuss with Ki."

"Those few things are the men you were talking to at the station?" Ki asked after Wright had gone.

"Yes," Jessie said, nodding. "I don't suppose you've ever run into them before?"

Ki had been inspecting the men on the station platform while Jessie talked. He shook his head. "Even at this distance I'm sure I could recognize them if I'd ever met them, Jessie. What are they here for?"

"I don't know yet. Their names—at least the names they gave me—are Jack Johnson and Tek Powell. And I hate to seem overly suspicious after talking with them only for a couple of minutes, but from the few words they said, I got the idea that they've come here with some kind of get-rich-quick scheme."

"They certainly wouldn't be the first," Ki commented.

"Or the last, if they really are confidence men," Jessie said with a smile. "But I'm not really inclined to listen to them. I certainly don't need any more money, and I'm sure they know that."

"What do you think they've come here for, then?"

"I can't imagine, unless they want to use me for bait."

"To draw the unwary?"

"Of course. You might say that the people they want to cheat are mice, and I'm supposed to be the piece of cheese that attracts them to the trap. I'm sure their real objective isn't as much to take my money as it is to get the Starbuck name attached to whatever cheating scheme they might be planning."

"They wouldn't be the first to try that, either."

"Of course not. But I resent being thought of or used as a piece of cheese, Ki."

"And I don't blame you. Have you decided what you'll tell them when they dangle their bait in front of you?"

"That's what I've been trying to make up my mind about ever since they gave me a hint of why they've come here. Right now, I'm half inclined to go along with whatever they propose. I'll find out what their scheme is, and at the right time I'll spring a trap myself and they'll be the ones caught in it."

"You'd probably save a lot of innocent people from being parted from their money if you did. But how are you going to work everything out?"

"I've thought about that, Ki. They certainly can't stay here at the depot, and I'm going to have to give them time to talk me into whatever scheme they're planning. I'll have to invite them to the Circle Star."

"That'll be easy to do," Ki suggested. "We've even got the spare horses for them, the ones Ed and Shorty were riding."

"Yes," Jessie said. "I took that into account. And I think I'll just go ahead and follow my plan, if you can call it that this early."

"Oh, I'm sure you're right, both in your ideas about what those fellows came here for, and your feeling that you'll save a lot of innocent people if you put those swindlers out of business or even in jail. What do you want me to do to help, Jessie?"

"Just follow my lead and let the swindlers think we're both being taken in," Jessie replied. "We'll play along with them until the time is right, then spring our own trap."

Back at the depot where Johnson and Powell were waiting, Jessie made a token apology for having had to leave them, then went on, "I'm sure you've realized by now that there aren't any kind of accommodations here at the depot. But if you gentlemen don't mind a fairly long horseback ride, I can put you up at the Circle Star for a day or two."

"Now, we don't want to put you to any extra trouble, Miss Starbuck," Johnson protested. "We thought there'd be a town here and a hotel where we could stay."

"Others have made the same mistake." Jessie smiled.

"Now, to get down to practical matters, two of my ranch hands went with the herd to Forth Worth, so we have two spare horses. I'm sure you're both at home on horseback?"

"Oh, of course," Powell said quickly.

"Let's consider it settled, then," Jessie told them. "I'll have one of the men lead the horses up here, and we'll start back to the Circle Star without losing any more time. By the time we get there, it'll be too late for us to do any talking, but tomorrow we'll sit down together, and I'll listen to whatever it is you've come to tell me about."

"It's real nice of you to take us in this way," Johnson said ingratiatingly, "And you sure won't lose anything by doing it. Once you hear what we've got to tell you, I think you'll agree with me."

Darkness had fallen long before the little cavalcade came in sight of the lights of the Circle Star's bunkhouse and kitchen. The main house was unlighted, and darkness also hid the bulk of the stables and storage sheds and the huge barn, as well as the horse corrals and the other facilities required to keep the vast ranch functioning. Lamps glowed in the bunkhouse and the cookhouse, but the light spilling from their windows dispelled only part of the night's gloom.

Gimpy, the cook, came out of the cookhouse when he heard the hoofbeats of the party. He carried a lantern, and lighted Jessie and Ki and their visitors to the main house.

"I got supper all ready for everbody, Miz Jessie," he told her. "Didn't figure you'd bring company back with you, but there's more'n enough to feed them, too. All I got to do is dish up and you can set down and eat."

"While we're waiting, I'll show you gentlemen to your bedroom," Ki volunteered. "I'm sure you'll want to freshen up before we sit down to supper."

Johnson nodded absently. He and his companion had been inspecting the luxurious formal parlor of the main house. It was a room that Jessie seldom used. Alex had assembled an array of choice English and French furniture to please Jessie's mother, but she had not lived to appreciate it, for death had taken her in giving birth to Jessie. The formal living room remained unused most of the time, for Jessie preferred the small study which had been Alex Starbuck's favorite room and was now her favorite because of the memories it held of her father.

"You got quite some layout here, Miss Starbuck," Johnson commented before turning with his companion to follow Ki upstairs to the bedroom Jessie had offered them. "I'd say the cattle business is pretty good right now."

"It's very satisfactory," Jessie nodded. "But we can talk business later, over the supper table. Or, better yet, we can wait until tomorrow. I'd imagine the day's been as busy and hurried for you as it has for Ki and me. We'll have a quick supper, and take up the purpose of your visit tomorrow."

"Well, Ki, what do you think of our guests?" Jessie asked as the two of them sat in the study after Johnson and Powell had left for their beds.

"I think your judgment of them hit the target square in the bullseye," Ki replied. "They're doing their best to act like businessmen, but they can't hide what they actually are. I'm sure they'll lay out some sort of confidence game for you when you talk with them tomorrow."

"I've got that same feeling," Jessie agreed. "And I'll listen to them carefully. You know how I feel about cheaters, Ki. If they expect to use the Starbuck name to swindle investors with worthless stock or anything of that sort, I feel right now that I'll go along with whatever scheme they trot out until we've got enough evidence to expose them."

Ki nodded, then stood up and said, "I'm going to bed now, myself. We'll have another private talk in the morning, Jessie, after you've found out what our unexpected guests are up to."

Left alone in the room that had been her father's favorite, Jessie snuggled down into the big armchair. Its smooth softly supple cordovan leather still carried a faint aroma of Alex's pipe tobacco. His life-sized portrait hung on one wall, facing a similar picture across the room of the mother Jessie had never known.

Alex's scarred and much-used oak rolltop desk was in one corner. It was the first desk he'd owned, one he'd bought when he started the small shop on the San Francisco waterfront, where he'd dealt in imported goods from the Far East. Though Jessie had never seen the store that had begun her father's meteoric business career, Ki had described it to her very vividly. He had been with Alex Starbuck almost from the start and had watched him rise from a small-time merchant to become one of the giants of American business and industry.

Within a short time after opening his store, Alex had found that dealing through middlemen in stocking his modest establishment was both unsatisfactory and time-consuming. He risked the loss of almost every dollar he'd earned by making a trip to the Orient. There he'd been able to make arrangements with exporters in both Japan and China to fill his orders direct, and his store had prospered because of the unique merchandise he was soon able to offer.

As his small business became a large importing firm, Alex had acquired a battered merchant ship to carry his cargoes. When the demands for his merchandise began to outstrip the capacity of his one battered vessel, he'd bought another. It needed extensive repairs, and when the small shipyard where he'd placed the vessel for refurbishing encountered financial difficulties, he'd offered to buy it from its aging owner.

To keep the shipyard busy, Alex went to other merchants who depended on Oriental imports and convinced them of the savings that could be made by owning their own vessels, and the shipyard prospered. At the height of the expansion being felt by the Western states, when railroads began pushing their tracks across the continent, Alex had been among the first to recognize the future of rail transport and had invested heavily in railroad stocks.

Their boom added solidity to his financial base, and he then expanded into the fields of finance, banking, and brokerage. At a very early age Alex had established himself as a man who was scrupulously honest as well as gifted with sound financial judgment. He began receiving invitations to join older and better-established financiers in their ventures, and by applying the shrewd appraisals he'd learned to make—for not all his ventures had been profitable—Alex became extremely wealthy while still a relatively young man.

Tragically for Jessie, his only child from a late marriage to the wife who'd died in childbirth, Alex's meteoric rise in the American business world also drew him to the attention of a cartel of European and Asiatic moguls who had watched with growing envy the growing wealth and power of industrial America. The cartel had been formed with one idea: to take control of the key businesses and financial resources of the entire North American continent.

While most business moguls in the United States scoffed at the idea that such a cartel could even be formed, much less exist without their knowing about it, Alex's connections in the Far East confirmed the cartel's aims. He started to fight the sinister group which operated in secrecy and sought to attain its ends by violence. In his battle against the cartel, Alex was aided by Ki.

Ki's life had been radically different from Alex's. Born in Japan, Ki was the son of an American naval officer and the daughter of a Japanese noble family. When their daughter married an American instead of one of the sons of the samurai, her parents disowned her. When both his father and mother perished in a storm at sea, Ki turned his back on his grandparents. He became a wanderer, and to earn his keep joined the *do* of Kirata, a master of Oriental martial arts.

When he'd acquired the necessary combat skills, Ki became a mercenary, wandering through the Orient and joining one or another of the constantly changing groups of the wealthy nobles which waged a continuing warfare against the established governments, seeking to acquire power for themselves.

In his wanderings Ki heard of Alex Starbuck from a geisha who'd once been attached to his parents' household, and knew of the strong friendship that had existed between Alex and Ki's father. Tired of his aimless life, Ki set out to find Alex and at last succeeded. Alex not only gave Ki a home. He made the intelligent young Oriental his good right hand, a confidential assistant on whom he also depended to protect him from the increasing attacks by the European cartel.

Chance in the form of a mortgage forfeiture brought Alex the bulk of the huge tract of land in Southwest Texas which became the Circle Star Ranch. On his first visit to inspect the thousands of acres of which he'd now unexpectedly become owner, Alex had fallen in love with the vast peaceful expanse of prairie and decided it was the place he wished to call home.

Jessie, a gangling schoolgirl when she first saw the beginning of the Circle Star, had also been drawn to the ranch her father was creating. She was at that time a student in a select New England girls' finishing academy and was only a few months from graduation when a small army of the European cartel's hired killers attacked the ranch and murdered her father.

Ki had been elsewhere on the Circle Star when the murderers struck. He could not forgive himself for his failure to be at Alex's side when the murderous gang struck, and had dedicated himself to Jessie's service. With the skill that had come to him from his Asiatic schooling in the martial arts and the affectionate gratitude he felt toward Alex for having saved him from an aimless life, Ki trod the narrow line of being Jessie's companion, protector, and friend, without interfering in her business decisions or interfering in her private life.

Jessie had given Ki a similar understanding. Following her mother's death in bringing her into the world, Alex had employed an aging geisha to be Jessie's nurse and childhood companion. Due to the constant attention and instruction given her by the wise old woman, Jessie had acquired knowledge that she was now putting to use, just as she'd put to use the knowledge passed on to her by Ki in holding on to Alex's industrial and financial empire and even enlarging it.

Now, in the big armchair that brought back memories of her father, Jessie felt the tensions of the past few busy days draining away. She wasted no time wondering what sort of scheme the two men sleeping upstairs had in mind; they were only the latest confidence men of the many get-rich-quick peddlers who'd plotted to get their hands on a part of the Starbuck fortune.

A spell of yawning suddenly caught Jessie, reminding her that the hour was late and that the past few days had been busy ones. Picking up the small night-lamp that stood on the table by the door, its wick already burning, Jessie blew out the other lamps and went upstairs to her bedroom.

At the big double window the curtains of the sparsely furnished chamber were billowing gently in the cool breeze that usually began sweeping across the Texas prairie soon after sunset. Jessie did not waste time lighting the other lamps that stood ready, but undressed by the faint glow of the night-lamp. She stood for a moment, letting the breeze waft over her magnificent body, then blew out the lamp and slipped into bed. In only a few moments she was sound asleep.

★

Chapter 3

A change in the temperature of her bedroom awakened Jessie. The cool breeze that had flowed gently and steadily through her bedroom's open windows during the hours of darkness was now changing rapidly, becoming warm and gusting fitfully. The windows of her bedroom no longer showed blank and dark. They were beginning to glow with the golden rays of the rising sun.

Jessie threw back the blanket which had been so welcome during the night and stepped to the Aubusson carpet that covered the bedroom's floor. She stood beside the bed for a moment, stretching and twisting her shoulders and flexing her arms and legs to get rid of the stiffness that a night's sound, motionless sleep had created. Then she moved briskly to the washstand and filled the washbowl from its pitcher. A quick efficient sponge bath brought her fully awake, and by the time she'd dressed and combed her luxuriant shoulder-length blond hair, she was more than ready to start downstairs to the dining room.

Just as Jessie reached the last step the front door swung open and Gimpy came in, followed by one of the cowhands. Both of them carried large trays with platters of fried potatoes, thin breakfast steaks, hot biscuits, syrup, and white-flour gravy. A coffeepot stood on one of the trays.

"Did I git here before you was ready for breakfast, Miss Jessie?" Gimpy asked when he saw Jessie.

"I—why, I really don't know," Jessie told him. "I'm just getting up, and I don't know about Ki and our guests."

Ki entered the hall just in time to hear the exchange between Jessie and the cook. He said, "Our guests are in the dining room, and I was just starting across to the cookshack to tell Gimpy we'd be glad to have some food as soon as he could get it ready."

"Me and Sam'll go on in and load the table, then," Gimpy said, jerking his head toward his helper.

Jessie made an almost imperceptible gesture to Ki as the two men started for the dining room. As they vanished with the trays, Jessie dropped her voice and asked Ki, "I don't suppose you've had time yet to talk to Johnson and Powell?"

"Nothing beyond a good-morning," Ki responded. "I knew that you'd be coming along soon, so I excused myself and told them I'd go over to the cookshack and find out when breakfast would be ready. I didn't want to start talking to them until you got to the table."

"Then let's go in and find out what their story is."

Jessie led the way into the dining room, Ki following close behind her. Johnson and Powell were standing at one of the wide windows, looking out over the bunkhouse and barns and sheds and corrals that formed the heart of the Circle Star. Beyond the buildings the rolling prairie stretched to the horizon, its grassy surface rippling gently in the light fresh morning breeze. They turned to face Jessie and Ki.

"Good morning," Jessie said. "I hope you slept well last night?"

"Neither one of us blinked an eye all night," Johnson replied. "It was real thoughtful of you to take us in, Miss Starbuck, not knowing either me nor Tek from Adam's off-ox."

"It sure was!" Powell seconded his companion. "And just from looking out the window here I can see you got quite some spread. I looked all over for a line fence, but I didn't see one anyplace."

"We don't run much to fences on the Circle Star," Jessie told him, gesturing toward the table as an invitation for the two men to sit down. "We do have a line fence and a few sections of fenced pasture that we use mostly at calving time. None of them are in sight of the main house here."

"But you can see a long way over the prairie," Powell went on. "And if you've got some whole sections fenced off—" He paused and Jessie could tell that he was doing some mental figuring. Then he said, "I've heard a little bit about your ranch here, but a section's ten by ten miles, Miss Starbuck. Just how big is this place of yours?"

"I suppose you'd have to call the Circle Star a big ranch, even by Texas measurement," she said, smiling. "Not as big as the XIT, up in the Panhandle—it takes in most of ten counties. But the Circle Star has all the room I need to run a fairly large cattle herd, and it's big enough to keep next-door neighbors from peering into our windows."

"I just imagine it would be!" Jackson said quickly. He turned to his companion and went on: "Don't you think that instead of bothering Miss Starbuck with a lot of questions about her ranch, we'd better see if she's ready to listen to us explain why we've come here to talk to her?"

Powell nodded. "If she don't mind us talking while we have breakfast, I guess this is as good a time as any." He looked across the table at Jessie and asked, "Do you have any objection, ma'am?"

"Not in the least," Jessie replied. "And I'll admit I'm a bit curious to find out why you came all the way here to Texas looking for me."

"Not meaning to hurt your feelings, Miss Starbuck, your ranch here is closer to where we happened to be than San Francisco is. We talked it over, who we'd take our proposition to first, and all of us agreed it oughta be you."

"And that's the only reason?" Jessie frowned. "You didn't know anything about me when you made up your minds?"

"Well, now," Johnson began, "I suppose everybody in the whole United States knows about your father, Miss Starbuck, what a successful businessman he was. And folks know how well you've done, taking over after a bunch of scoundrels murdered him. And somehow your name kept popping up when me and Tek and our other partner, Hap Benson, were talking about what we need. So that's the reason we've come to see you."

Keeping her voice carefully neutral, when Johnson fell silent, Jessie said, "You want me to join you in this venture you mentioned, Mr. Johnson?"

"That's about the size of it."

Jessie frowned. "You must know I have my own business interests that require fairly constant attention."

"Oh, sure. That's one of the big reasons we've come to talk with you," Johnson answered. "But the men that're in on this deal I was starting to tell you about don't have big names, like Huntington and Hopkins and Stanford and Crocker. Or, when you come down to it, like Starbuck."

"I see," Jessie nodded. "What you're saying is that you don't really want me to join you in this business venture you're trying to start. All that you really want is the use of my name. Am I right?"

"Now, that's not the way of it at all, Miss Starbuck!" Powell protested. He'd started his denial almost before Jessie finished speaking. "Jack and Hap and me're smart enough to know that we can't swing a deal big as this one is by ourselves. That's why we went looking for partners in the first place."

"Then did you just come to offer stock in your proposition?" Jessie pressed. "Because if you did, I can save all three of us a great deal of time. I don't buy stock in any but the biggest and best-established companies, gentlemen. And let me assure you that I choose them very, very carefully."

"Well, there'd be some stock-buying in this deal we got in mind to offer you," Johnson admitted. He spoke slowly and carefully, as though choosing each word with the utmost precision. "But there'll be plenty of land bought with the money we'd get from selling the stock. It'd be enough land to be good for whatever the stock sold for and a lot more than that by the time we'd've done a little bit of work on it."

Jessie had already decided that the two men were

promoters who'd come to her touting some sort of marginal, perhaps even crooked scheme. Still, her curiosity led her to ask, "I assume this would be freehold land, with a completely clear title?"

"It sure as h—" Johnson cut his reply short before the bit of profanity slipped out. He took a fresh breath and went on smoothly: "It'd be clear land, Miss Starbuck. Bought direct from the United States Government. I don't guess you'd want a better title to it than that."

"Did you come to me because this land is in Texas?" Jessie asked with a frown. In spite of the *CAUTION!* flags waving in her mind she could not hold back her curiosity. "I suppose you know that because Texas was owned—or claimed—by Spain and France and Mexico, clear land titles here are very often quite hard to get and sometimes what seems to be a clear title turns out to be clouded."

Johnson and Powell both nodded, then Johnson went on, his voice filled with assurance: "We're not one bit worried about getting a clear land title. I'll tell you now in strict confidence that we'll be buying public land in Arizona Territory."

"And what makes this land so valuable?" Jessie asked.

Johnson did not answer immediately. Instead he glanced at Powell, his eyebrows now raised in a silent question.

"I guess it's all right, Jack," Powell said slowly. "We've got to tell somebody sooner or later, and we might as well start with Miss Starbuck. You and me and Hap talked about this thing enough to know he won't mind."

"Hap?" Jessie frowned. "You mentioned that name before, but I'm not quite sure what part he has in all this."

Before Johnson had a chance to speak, Powell replied for him. "Hap Benson," he told Jessie. "He's our other partner. He stayed back in Arizona to keep an eye on things while we come here to talk to you."

Jessie sat in silence for a moment after Powell finished his explanation. Then she said, "You gentlemen have obviously made some sort of discovery on this land you've mentioned. I suppose it's minerals, since I've traveled over a great deal of Arizona Territory and haven't seen a great deal of good rangeland or land that would be suitable for farming. Am I right in assuming this much?"

"Right as rain," Johnson said, nodding. "And since it's pretty much public knowledge that you inherited several mining properties from your father, Miss Starbuck, Jack and Hap Benson and me are all of the same mind. We've got the richest lode this country's ever seen, but we're going to need cash to get anything out of it."

"And that's where I come in," Jessie said quickly when Johnson paused for breath. "You're looking for investors, I'm sure."

"You hit the nail square on the head," Powell said.

"Why me?" Jessie asked. "There are stock exchanges in San Francisco and New York and Chicago that sell mining stocks. Why haven't you gone to one of them?"

"Because we don't want too many people nuzzling up to the trough when payoff time comes around," Powell replied without hesitation. "Me and Tek and Hap Benson put our heads together and talked things over before we did anything else. All of us figure we'll be better off if we just split our stock three or four ways instead of three or four hundred, maybe a whole lot more."

"Other new companies put their stock on the market to get the capital they need," Jessie reminded him.

"But we ain't other companies!" Johnson broke in quickly.

Jessie noticed how suddenly his carefully cultivated manner of speaking changed. She said nothing and kept a straight face but smiled inwardly as he went on.

"I guess you learned about how the stock market works and things like that from your daddy, Miss Starbuck. Me and Tek wasn't that lucky. Ours didn't teach us anything of that kind."

"None of the Starbuck companies has any stock sold through the exchange," Jessie assured Johnson. "And I don't buy stock in other companies for speculation. But suppose you finish your explanation of this tremendously rich lode you mentioned. Is it gold? Silver? Copper?"

"Not any of those," Johnson replied. "It's diamonds."

For a moment Jessie could only stare incredulously at the two men. Then she regained her poise. Keeping her voice expressionless, she said, "There are no diamond deposits on the North American continent, Mr. Johnson."

His voice quiet and obviously carefully controlled, Johnson replied, "Begging your pardon in advance, Miss Starbuck, I got to say you're wrong. What you ought've said was that up till now nobody's ever found any here in this country before."

"I'm sure I'd have heard about such a discovery, if one has been made," Jessie said firmly. "Men have been looking for diamonds since this country was settled, and that was more than two hundred years ago, but nobody has found any. I understand through some of the companies I do business with in connection with the Starbuck mines that a new diamond field was opened in Brazil several years ago, but that's the closest place to North America that any diamonds have been found."

"Sure, I heard about that," Johnson said. "I understand the diamonds they dig down there ain't real good grade, like the ones that come from Africa."

"So I've heard," Jessie said. "Which doesn't mean there won't be better stones uncovered in Brazil as the mines expand."

"Oh, sure," Johnson said. "But all we're doing right now, you and me, is beating around the bush."

"I'm afraid I'll have to agree with you," Jessie said. "And I apologize for breaking into your story. Please go on and tell me all the details you feel free to disclose."

"Well, it ain't much of a story," Johnson began. "Tek and Hap Benson and me was partnering in Arizona Territory, looking for copper. What we wound up finding was this diamond field I've been telling you about. We didn't believe it at first, any more than you do right now. Then, after we took a few stones to San Francisco and had a good jewelry man look at 'em, and he said they were good high-grade diamonds, we changed our minds."

"I suppose you have his report in writing?" Jessie broke in. "If you have, I'd—"

Johnson interrupted her. His voice quietly controlled, he said, "I'll get around to that in good time. If it's the truth you're looking for, I'm telling it to you right now, Miss Starbuck."

"Do go on," Jessie said.

"Well," he continued, "we scouted that valley, and I'll tell you right now, we went over it closer'n a fine-tooth comb would've done. And we found some more diamonds."

"Without digging for them?"

"Oh, we dug a few test-holes where the diamonds were the thickest. And from what we found, I'd bet we hit on five or six places where it'd pay to sink a shaft."

"But you didn't?"

"No, ma'am. Not a real shaft, just holes five or six feet deep. But that was as far as we needed to go. We took out enough raw diamonds to find out that it's a real rich field, Miss Starbuck."

"I see," Jessie said thoughtfully, then she went on, "I'm curious about something."

"What's that?" Powell asked.

"If this field is as rich as you say it is, why didn't you three just dig up a hatful of raw diamonds and sell them to cover your cost of developing it the way you want to? Why come to me—or anyone else, for that matter—looking for financing?"

"We talked about doing just that," Powell told her. "And the only reason we didn't go ahead the way you asked about is because we figured that since we don't own the land yet all the diamonds we'd dig would belong to the government."

"That's gospel fact," Johnson seconded. "If we took any diamonds away before we own the land they come from, all we'd be is plain old everyday thieves."

Jessie's first thought was that swindling by selling

worthless stock was just another form of theft, but she did not pass on her reaction to her visitors.

"I suppose that's true," she agreed. "But as I recall the prospecting laws, it's not a crime to take ore samples from land that belongs to the government if the only reason for taking them is to have an assay made to determine the value of a mineral deposit."

"Oh, that's the law, all right," Powell agreed quickly. "But there's something else Jack didn't mention. Government assay offices are like a sieve, Miss Starbuck. Maybe you know that?"

"I've heard them described that way before," she said, nodding.

"Well, then," Powell went on, "the minute a prospector files an assay in a government office, it's public property. Then every son of—" He stopped short for a moment, then went on: "Everybody and anybody can get a look at it. Then the first thing you know, there's a rush to wherever the assay samples came from."

Johnson chimed in quickly, "And once the cat's outa the bag, there's no putting it back, Miss Starbuck. I reckon you know that. We aim to keep this find we made absolutely secret until we've got the land all around it tied up for ourselves."

"I'm not even going to ask you where this discovery you've been telling me about is located," Jessie assured him. "And I'm not going to make up my mind about your proposition until I've had some time to think about it."

"How much time you figure it'll take you?" Powell asked.

"Not too long. A day or so at most," Jessie replied. "I'll want to talk about it with Ki and do some thinking myself, as I've just said. And of course I'll want you to give me some estimate of the amount of money that you'll need to start working this deposit you've found."

"We've already done some talking about that, all three of us," Johnson said quickly. "Whenever you want to look at them, I'll sure be glad to go over 'em with you."

"Later today," Jessie said. "There are a few things that Ki and I will need to attend to now that we're back. For one thing, my foreman has gone to Fort Worth with the market herd, and I want to be sure that the man who'll be taking over the job until he gets back knows exactly what has to be done."

"Sure, we understand about that," Johnson said, nodding. "Tek and me will just sorta make ourselves scarce and keep out from underfoot while you're taking care of whatever you got to do."

"This afternoon," Jessie said. "And in the meantime, just make yourselves at home."

"Oh, we'll manage," Powell assured her. "And I sure hope you can figure out a way to join in with us."

"We'll just have to wait and see," Jessie said. "But the morning's slipping away from us while we sit here talking." She stood up and turned to Ki. "Let's spend a few minutes together in the study, Ki. There are several things we need to talk about before we do anything else."

"Well?" Jessie asked Ki as she closed the door of the study behind them. "Did you come to the same conclusion I did?"

"I'm sure I did," he said, nodding. "They're con men, all right, just as we'd suspected. But there's something else that came to mind while they were spinning their yarn to us, Jessie."

"Something about Johnson and Powell?"

Ki shook his head. "I've never heard of them before, any more than you have. No, Jessie. What I remembered was that Alex had almost the same proposition offered him once, and he spent some time investigating it before he turned it down."

"You don't remember any of the details?"

"No. And unfortunately, I don't remember exactly when the offer was made. At the time I wasn't as familiar with Alex's business affairs as I came to be later on, after he had more confidence in me. But I'm sure there'll be some reference to the proposition he was offered, somewhere in his diaries or his day books."

"Then suppose I just shut myself up in here and go over the records that Alex kept?" Jessie suggested. "You can take care of the odds and ends that the men might forget to attend to with Ed away. And you can keep an eye on our guests while I'm doing my digging into the past."

★

Chapter 4

Alone in the study, Jessie went to the battered rolltop desk that had belonged to her father. The desk was a large one, crafted of oak. Its top was as high as Jessie's shoulders as she rolled back its cover and gazed at the packed pigeonholes that lined its back above the rectangle of fine glazed leather that covered its writing area.

During the first years that followed Alex's murder, Jessie had avoided the desk; its very presence reminded her of him and of his busy, productive life. Then as the pain and shock of his death ebbed, the sense of finality it had brought her grew no less painful, but she'd learned to accept it. Then, as she came into contact more and more closely with the far-flung industrial and financial empire that had been Alex's legacy, Jessie had made a start at sorting and arranging his papers in chronological order.

Sheaves of papers neatly stacked and tied into neat bundles with stenographer's tape took up the bottom surface of the triangular-shaped top compartment. Bundles of letters filled most of the pigeonholes that rose in tiers from the writing surface; the exception was a horizontal line of pigeonholes near the top, these contained the dozens of pocket-sized memorandum booklets in which Alex had jotted down appointments as well as memoranda.

Unlike the dairies he'd kept, which Jessie had put into the deep drawers on each pedestal, Alex's notes were pithy. It had been his habit, following the date and time of an appointment, to enter brief memos of the key points that had been settled during his conversations with the financial moguls and to jot down the key words that described a transaction involving land or goods or business holdings or stocks which had resulted from the handshake-settled agreements.

Jessie had not yet read all the pages of every notebook, but she was positive that she'd seen no mention of a gold-mining deal in any of those she'd gone through earlier. Settling into the swivel-chair which stood in front of the desk, Jessie began thumbing through the notebooks, looking for a starting point. She started her search with the notebook at the point where she'd stopped when she'd last looked through the little books some months earlier.

Since the cover of each book bore in gold-leaf embossing the month and year in which it had been used, it had been an easy job to arrange them by dates. Now Jessie scanned through the first of them very quickly, looking for any jotted memoranda that might give her a clue to the incident which Ki had mentioned. The first book had contained no entries that were helpful, nor did the next two. Then, in the fourth book, she found what she'd been seeking.

She'd gone halfway through the little notebook when

on the bottom line of a page she found a brief entry in Alex's bold handwriting. It read: "Diamonds. M. S. Latham. Lunch, 12:30, St. Francis Htl."

Jessie was familiar with Latham's name. When she'd first encountered it, she'd asked Ki about the name, and he'd remembered that the man referred to was a San Francisco attorney who represented a number of wealthy clients, including the Gurneys, one of England's richest families. Jessie turned the page quickly. As she'd hoped but had been half-afraid to expect, the next two pages were filled with notes of the subject that Alex and Latham had gone into during their luncheon.

Most of Alex's quick jottings defied Jessie's first efforts to decipher them, but one yielded to her attempt very quickly. In its original form as jotted down by Alex during his luncheon conversation with Latham, it read: "G's inc Blumefontain M. = 2 mil BPS yr." Jessie's retentive mind recalled Alex's habits in abbreviating and she translated the entry as "Gurney's income from Blumefontain Mines is two million British pounds sterling per year."

Another scribble on the following page also gave up its secret, when Jessie deciphered it as meaning that Latham had predicted that shares in the investment group Latham was forming to exploit the first discovery of diamonds in the United States could be expected to return ten thousand dollars per year for each dollar invested.

Then, when Jessie turned the page, she encountered two yellowed newspaper clippings that had been neatly folded to fit inside the little notebook. Handling the brittle paper very carefully, she unfolded one. With his usual care, Alex had cut out the item to include the line identifying the newspaper. The clipping had been taken from the July 10, 1871 issue of the daily *Alta Californian,* one of San Francisco's first newspapers. Written by a "special correspondent" identifying himself as the "Old Prospector," the item read:

Articles of Incorporation are rumored ready to be filed soon by a financial consortium whose members do not wish to be identified at the time of this writing. The group is in process of its formation, and among its members are expected to be nabobs such as A. Gansel, M. G. King, G. D. Roberts, A. Starbuck, Chauncey Fairfield, M. S. Latham, and others.

Messrs. Gansel and Latham are known to represent British financiers strongly identified as being in the diamond trade, and Mr. Starbuck is also known for his mining ventures. The rumors have it that the discovery of an immense diamond deposit in the Western United States has brought the consortium together.

Mr. Henry Janin, the well-known geologist, is believed to have certified that samples taken from the extensive deposits are genuine diamonds of the finest gem quality.

Gently smoothing out the second fragile clipping, which was several times as long as the first and dated October 2, 1872, Jessie began reading:

From the Diamond Fields—About the 20th of August a party of men left this city to explore the diamond fields about which there has been such a furor of excitement. Amongst them were the following well-known gentlemen: G. D. Roberts, General John W. Bost, M. G. King, M. G. Gillette, Alfred Rubery, John F. Boyd, Dr. C. Cleveland, E. M. Fry, Chauncey Fairfield, and Chas. G. Myers.

The members of the expedition returned last evening. They experienced no trouble with the Indians, but had a very tedious march to the fields and thence home. The heads of the party declare that their explorations more than confirmed the original report of Mr. Janin of the extent and richness of the deposits, and they exhibited specimens which they say they secured with their own exertions and but little labor. This party went merely to explore and prospect the country where the diamonds and rubies were said to abound and not for the purpose of working. They say that operations could not be carried on when they were there, as the altitude is great and the ground covered with snow. The specimens they brought back are similar to those previously exhibited in this city, and they number 286 diamonds of various sizes.

Mr. Roberts says that if they had been deceived, they are the worst deceived and cheated men who ever lived. They surveyed 3,000 acres of land and propose to keep secret the exact locality until the company receives a Government patent. The implements used by them seem to have been ordinary jackknives—an improvement on the boot heels of the original locators.

If so much wealth can be turned up by such

primitive means, what might be accomplished with shovels and pickaxes? The report of the party renewed the excitement and little else is talked about on California Street but diamonds and rubies. A meeting of the trustees of the company was called for 2 p.m., and further developments will be awaited with interest. A fact that is so easily demonstrated as the existence of diamonds in that country should not be longer one of doubt and suspicion.

After she'd refolded the brittle yellowing strip of newsprint, Jessie replaced it in the little pocket-sized notebook and restored the book to its place. She leafed on through the books that remained, but even the cursory examination she gave them showed that there was no further reference to diamonds or diamond mining.

A moment's pondering gave Jessie the answer: the excitement over diamonds being discovered in North America, and especially in the West, had not seized Alex with the viselike grip with which it held other Western financial giants. Those most deeply afflicted with the diamond frenzy had primarily been investors, men who'd made their fortunes in the legal or medical professions or in banking or some other enterprise into which they'd placed knowledge and funds, but had not been participants.

Alex, on the other hand, had earned his fortune by taking an active part in developing shipping, mining, ranching, timber-cutting, and all the other solid foundations on which the Starbuck wealth had been built. He had been in the front line of progress, not in the rear ranks using only his mind and money to increase his wealth. Jessie nodded with satisfaction at her solution, then closed the desk and went out to find Ki.

"I've been doing a lot of thinking back since our talk this morning," Ki told her after he'd listened to Jessie's quick summary of what she'd discovered. "And I've remembered a few things that I haven't thought about in a long time."

"About the diamond fields?"

Ki smiled. "Those diamond fields were created by a bunch of crooks and confidence men, Jessie. They simply bought several pounds of uncut diamonds and salted a valley in the Arizona desert with them. It didn't take long before somebody caught on to their scheme and exposed them."

"Then those newspaper clippings must have been the first news reports to appear," Jessie said, frowning. "I wondered why they were so—well, so vague. Who caught up with them?"

"Those prominent men who'd invested in the diamond swindle weren't total fools, Jessie," Ki said. "I remember now how the swindle was exposed. Some of them insisted on sending all the diamonds to New York, to get them appraised by Charles Tiffany. He was a real expert—he could tell where a diamond came from just by looking at it closely."

"I've never been a great admirer of jewelry, Ki. You know that. I didn't know that an expert could tell where a diamond came from."

"Well, Mr. Tiffany could. As I recall, he also found a few rubies and some sapphires among the diamonds, and they're stones that never are found in diamond-producing areas."

"What happened to the group that was going to operate the diamond mines? Alex's diaries don't have a word about that."

"Oh, they just kept quiet until the town stopped laughing at them. Then I assume they dissolved their corporation—or it may be that they just didn't finish organizing it. All they'd have had to do was to avoid registering it in Sacramento."

"Yes, of course," she said, nodding. "And things of that sort tend to fade away and be forgotten. I suppose that must be what happened."

"I hadn't been with Alex too long at that time," Ki went on. "But the men who'd been promoting it couldn't have been very proud of themselves, and they had enough power to smother a lot of what happened."

"Apparently they had enough power to keep any more mention of it out of the newspapers later on," Jessie said. "Those two clippings were the only ones I found, and I went through all the rest of Alex's old memorandum books looking for more."

"It seems to me you've found out all we needed to know," Ki said with a frown. "Now you'll have to decide how to handle this new bunch that's trying to start a new diamond swindle."

Jessie's voice was thoughtful as she said, "I think I've already decided that, Ki. If I turn them down they'll just go looking for somebody else. Whomever they pick for their next victim might not know about the first one, and confidence men as shrewd as Johnson and Powell can be very persuasive."

"Then you're going to pretend to go along with them?"

"Yes. I'm sure they'll want me to put some money

into their scheme, but it's money I can afford to lose. I can't think of a better way to spend it than putting these men in jail."

"Do you have a plan, Jessie?"

"Not yet. There'll be plenty of time to plan, Ki. There are a lot of things we don't know yet about what the swindlers are going to come up with."

"You can almost guess that," Ki said, frowning. "They'll have some kind of plausible story about discovering diamonds in some out-of-the-way spot. Then I imagine they'll bring out a few samples, more than likely a handful of uncut diamonds. Finally, they'll tell you how rich you'll be if you finance them in mining the diamonds, but as soon as possible after they've persuaded you, they'll disappear and take your money with them."

Jessie nodded. "Yes, I'm sure you're right. But let's give them a free rein, and as soon as we learn what they intend to do, we'll work out a way to get the evidence we need to put them behind bars."

"I suppose you intend to start right away?"

"I don't think I'll have to do a thing, Ki. They'll do the starting themselves. The first chance they'll have will be when we're having our noon meal. I'm sure that all we'll have to do is listen and open our eyes wide and go along with whatever they suggest."

Jessie's prediction proved to be accurate. She stayed in the study through the remainder of the morning, purposely avoiding Johnson and Powell. She was certain that they'd become a bit impatient to start their scheme working, and was standing in front of the main house watching for her guests when Gimpy beat the triangle to call the Circle Star hands to lunch. Johnson and Powell made their appearance soon enough, mingling with the ranch hands heading for the cookshack. Jessie motioned for them to join her.

"I'm sorry I haven't been able to join you until now," she said. "But there are always a lot of letters and reports and things of that sort that I have to take care of."

"Oh, we understand that," Powell said. "A big ranch like this one's bound to mean a lot of work."

"We're not a bit put out, Miss Starbuck," Johnson chimed in. "Maybe you'll have a chance to listen to what we need to talk about while we're eating."

"I'm sure we will," Jessie replied. "In fact, that's just what I'd planned on. I've been—well, I suppose you'd say that the idea of American diamond mining has caught my imagination."

Before either of the two could reply, Gimpy stuck his head out of the cookshack door. "Miss Jessie!" he called. "If you and your friends're ready to set down, I'll bring your grub across before I start dishing up f'r the boys. They're sorta straggling in today, so it'll suit me just as good t'git you folks took care of fust."

"That'll be fine, Gimpy," Jessie said. "Whenever you get over here, we'll be ready to sit down."

Ki made his appearance in time to hear the last part of the exchange between Jessie and the cook. He hurried to join Jessie and the diamond touters, and gave Gimpy a hand with the two trays of food that the cook was balancing precariously as he walked across the short space between the main house and the cookshack. Once the platters of steak and potatoes and biscuits and gravy had been placed on the table, and Gimpy had left to return to the cookshack, Johnson started talking.

"I'm sure you'll understand that we're not trying to hurry you, Miss Starbuck," he began. "But Tek and I can't stay away from the diamond deposit too long. Even with Hap Benson there to guard the claim we've staked, there are people around who'd stop at nothing if they thought they had a chance to take that claim away from us."

"Oh, I understand," Jessie replied. "I've heard all about the outlaws who are always prowling around looking for loot. But I still haven't seen any diamonds from this claim you're talking about."

"We can satisfy you on that end of things real fast," Johnson said.

He took a bulging chamois pouch from his coat pocket and opened the drawstrings. Leaning across the table, he upended the pouch and emptied a stream of what at first glance appeared to be dully glistening whitish pebbles on the table in front of Jessie. For a moment Jessie said nothing, but leaned forward in her chair and gazed at the twenty or more stones.

"I don't recall ever having seen an uncut diamond before," she said slowly, a small frown forming on her face. "How am I to tell that these are real diamonds?"

"Oh, they're real enough, all right," Tek Powell assured her. "And fine-graded ones, too. Now, you'll just have to take our word about 'em being good grade, but we can show you right this minute that they're diamonds for sure, if you don't mind a few little scratches on one of your water glasses or on a windowpane."

"I do know that diamonds cut glass, Mr. Powell," Jessie said. "If you're going to give me a demonstration, I'd rather have you use one of the glasses on the table. Here on the ranch they're much easier to replace than windowpanes."

"Glass is glass," Johnson remarked as he picked up the unfilled water tumbler that stood beside his plate. He turned to Jessie and went on: "Pick up any of the stones on the table, Miss Starbuck. Take two or three or any number you want to. I'm asking you to choose, because if Tek or me was to do it you might figure we'd be running in a ringer on you, if you know what I mean."

"Yes, I do know the expression," Jessie said, nodding as she surveyed the scattered array of stones that Johnson had spilled from the pouch.

She picked one of them up and handed it to Johnson. He lifted the empty water tumbler that stood beside his plate and then held the stone Jessie had selected to the light, turning it as he examined it closely.

"If you're wondering why I'm doing this, it's to find a bump or an angle on the diamond," he explained. "The facets on a stone that's been cut and polished leave sharp edges, but when you're cutting glass with an uncut diamond you've got to find a bump or crack or edge of some sort." He was silent for a moment, continuing his inspection, then he went on: "Here's a little jaggedy bump on this one. Now I'll prove it's a diamond."

Upending the tumbler in front of him, Johnson gripped the stone firmly between his thumb and forefingers and brought it down the slanting side of the upturned glass. A small squeaking noise accompanied the stone's descent on the tumbler, and as Jessie and Ki watched a fine white line formed behind the descending stone.

Johnson pulled his hand away from the water glass when the scratch reached a length of almost two inches.

He picked up the tumbler and handed it to Jessie.

"Look at the line I've made," he said. "And feel it. Then cut a line for yourself, if you care to. Tek and me want you to be absolutely sure that every stone out of that pouch is a real, genuine diamond. And after you're satisfied, then maybe you'll feel like talking business with us."

★

Chapter 5

While Johnson was speaking, Jessie had been examining both the tumbler and the stone he'd handed her. She ran her fingertips along the line she'd seen inscribed on the tumbler, and could feel its almost infinitesimally rough edges.

"After your demonstration I don't have any doubt that this is a real diamond," she told Johnson. "But I know you won't mind if I try it myself."

"Of course not. That's what I expected you to do. Go right ahead," he replied.

Jessie placed the tumbler on the table and gripped the rough diamond firmly, then began scraping it down the side of the glass. At first the rough diamond left nothing but a wide smeared line on the smooth glass surface, then, as she grew accustomed to gripping it, a narrow whitish streak followed the stone as she scraped it slowly down the tumbler's side.

When the streak was an inch long, Jessie laid the diamond down and picked up the water glass. Holding it to the light that streamed through the window, she could see clearly the streak she'd created and the small fine line made by Johnson. She turned and offered the tumbler and stone to Ki.

"Wouldn't you like to try?" she asked.

"Of course," he said. "But with a different stone, if our guests have no objection."

"We don't mind one bit," Powell said quickly. "Pick up just whichever one of them stones you like. If you're of a mind to, you can try every last one of 'em, but before you run out you'd have a lot of Miss Starbuck's water glasses all marked up."

"That doesn't bother me a bit," Jessie put in. "In fact, even if window glass is hard to come by, when Ki's finished, I might try another stone on one of these panes."

"It'll leave a mark," Powell promised. "Just like every last one of them laying on this table will."

"Oh, I don't doubt that all the stones you put out there are genuine diamonds," Jessie said quickly. "And I'm willing to admit that I'm getting more and more interested in finding out about the place where you discovered them."

"Well, now, Miss Starbuck, that place is one of the things we came here to talk to you about," Johnson said. "It's sorta hard to tell about, because nobody believes that there's diamonds under the ground in this country, let alone them being the way they are in this canyon we found."

"Buried very shallowly?" Jessie asked, deciding that a bit of prompting might get them to the point of action faster.

"So shallow you won't believe it till you see the place!" Tek said enthusiastically. "Some of 'em poking out above ground, even. We didn't do much digging at all to gather up this bunch we brought along with us."

"Did you dig a shaft, to find out whether the underground deposits are as large as those near the surface?" Ki asked.

"We dug some, but I wouldn't say we put down a shaft," Tek replied. "We figure to do that later, after we've worked the surface good."

"We never did go more than knee-deep," Johnson added. He indicated the sample stones that he'd strewn on the table. "I'd say we dug up a good half of these, but we never did have to dig more than a ditch to find more."

"Then diamond mining in that place would be more like placer mining than anything else," Ki said thoughtfully.

"That's right!" Tek agreed. "No need for water, though, which is a good thing, because water's scarce there."

"All we did was shake the dirt through a sieve," Johnson volunteered. "We never did trench more'n knee-deep, and we were still finding stones when we stopped digging."

"We stopped mainly because we figured we'd got enough diamonds to show the kind of lode we'd struck," Tek explained. "Once we seen what we'd lucked into, we was in a sorta hurry to get that land wrapped up in a claim."

"And did you?" Jessie asked.

"Not right then," Johnson admitted. "Once we wore off the edge of what we'd stumbled into, and did some talking, we decided that we didn't need to be in all that much of a hurry."

"And we seen we'd be better off getting organized so we could work the field right," Johnson went on. "That's when one of us—I don't rightly recall which it was—but that's when somebody said 'Starbuck.' But now that we've found you and sorta got acquainted, it's easy to see we didn't make no mistake. You don't strike me as being a lady that takes forever and a day to make up her mind."

"I'm not," Jessie agreed. Her last exchanges with the two men had convinced her that she'd have nothing to gain by delaying the moment when the preliminaries could be pushed aside. She was sure now that she'd have no trouble getting the confidence men to reveal the full details of their scheme.

She went on: "I'm sure that you came here looking for a someone who's willing to put up the money—or maybe only part of it—to back you and your third partner in buying the land around this diamond field you've uncovered, and finding buyers for the diamonds."

Johnson nodded and turned to his partner. "You see?" he said. "I told you Miss Starbuck's the kind of smart lady that knows a good thing when somebody shows it to her."

"Then let's don't waste no more time shilly-shallying," Powell suggested. He turned to Jessie and went on: "If it's facts and figures you want, Miss Starbuck, we got all of 'em. You ask us whatever you feel like you need to know, and we'll sure tell you."

Jessie had her reply framed and ready. She said, "The first thing I want to know is where this diamond field is."

"Now, that's the one thing we can't let out," Johnson

answered unhesitatingly. "Not even to you, Miss Starbuck. It's not that we don't trust you, but there's others that might pick up a hint that you didn't even know you were giving out. Besides that, if you knew where to find the diamonds, you wouldn't need me and Tek any longer."

When Johnson paused, Tek took up where he'd left off. "You could just go file a claim for yourself. Not that I'm saying you'd be one to play a trick like that on somebody that had trusted you—but me and Jack and Hap Bensen would be out in the cold without a leg to stand on or a shoe to put on it if we had one."

Powell broke in to add, "We know how the mining claims law works, Miss Starbuck. We don't dare to talk too much, not even to somebody that's as honest as we figure you to be."

"Yes, I can understand why you'd feel you need to be protected against losing your claim, or having someone else file on the land before you're ready to do it," Jessie nodded. "And I'm sure you've figured out a way to protect yourself. Suppose you tell me what you suggest. I'd like to be sure that your plan—whatever it might happen to be—will protect me as well as it does you."

"What we figured out is to go to a bank," Johnson said. "A bank somewhere handy to where the diamonds are. We'll open us up a trustee account. I reckon you know what that is?"

"Of course," Jessie said. "The bank will be required by our instructions to pay the money out of the account only when all of us are there together to receive it."

Johnson turned to his partner to say, "You see, Tek? I told you and Hap that Miss Starbuck would know about trustee accounts. She'll put the money she's advancing us in one of them, and all of us will have to be there or have our names on a release before the bank will pay out a penny."

For a moment Jessie was tempted to point out that Johnson's description of a trustee account was not quite complete. Swindlers had a way of persuading their victims that no withdrawals could be made from a trustee account without consent of all the individuals in whose names the account had been opened. However, a name—even the Starbuck name—could very easily be forged on a check or a withdrawal slip which the unsuspecting bank would be required to honor, even though the amount called for might take every penny from the account and close it completely.

Jessie had no intention at this point of going into the details of any sort of transaction with the two men and their still-unknown third partner. She said, "Even before I think about your suggestion of a trustee account, Mr. Johnson, I'm going to need more than just your word and those of your partners that this diamond field is really all you've described it to be."

"Meaning what, Miss Starbuck?"

"Meaning that I'll want to see it and make sure that it's all you say it is," Jessie replied.

"We sure don't have nothing to hide," Tek said. "You can go along with us when we start back. You'll need somebody to show you the way, anyhow."

"Unfortunately, I can't leave the Circle Star for several days," Jessie told him. "We've been so busy gathering the market herd and getting it loaded on the train that I've fallen a bit behind with several things that concern my other business interests. I'll be busy for several days on work that needs my immediate attention."

Johnson frowned. "I guess we could wait a few days before we start back—if it wouldn't put you out having us here."

"You're welcome to stay, of course," Jessie offered. "Or, if you're in a big hurry to get back, just tell me how to find your claim, and Ki and I will join you there."

"It's not an easy place to find," Johnson said, his frown deepening. "You're sure you want to take the trouble of making a long trip—"

"Oh, I'm sure," Jessie replied. She kept her voice in an off-hand tone. "It's like buying a horse, Mr. Johnson. If the animal's covered with a saddle blanket, there's no way to tell whether or not it's got a sore back."

"Except that we're not horse-trading, Miss Starbuck," Tek put in. "Once you find out where that diamond field is, you don't even need to talk to the three of us any longer. Why, up alongside all the money you can spend hiring fancy lawyers and such, you could cut us off at the knees without half-trying."

"I suppose that's true, but I don't do business that way," Jessie said.

"Oh, I didn't mean you'd do a thing like that," Tek protested. "But we still got to—"

"Hold on, Tek," Johnson broke in. "There's an easy way to settle this." He turned to Jessie and went on: "We don't object a minute if you want to see that diamond field, Miss Starbuck. Now, if you don't mind being a mite uncomfortable for a pretty good while, I got an idea that'll get us started on this deal without wasting an awful lot of time."

"I'm quite ready to listen to anything reasonable,"

Jessie said. "But I'm curious to hear you explain why I'd have to be uncomfortable for a while."

"Well, to get to the place where we found the diamonds, you have to take a stagecoach from wherever traffic stops on that new Southern Pacific line they're pushing across the south part of the territory. Then you take the stagecoach to Gila Bend, and it won't be the most comfortable ride you've ever had, because the road's pretty rough. But one of us will meet you there and guide you the rest of the way."

"Where do we get on the stagecoach?" Ki asked.

"Unless they've jumped the railhead beyond it, you'll likely have to change to the stage at Casa Grande. It runs to three or four little towns, and Gila Bend's one of 'em. Gila Bend's not much of a town, just a little wide spot on the old southern Arizona stagecoach road, where the road crosses the Gila River. You'll know it because it's close to a big pile of adobe bricks from some old Indian pueblo that's all tumbled down."

"I'm sure we can find it without any trouble," Jessie said.

"But you'll still have a day's ride to the place where we found the diamonds," Johnson told her. "Now, let's say we fix up our spring wagon with a tarpaulin stretched over the bed, and you ride under the tarp from the stagecoach stop to our diamond claim. How does that strike you?"

"I'd only have one objection," Jessie replied. "I wouldn't be able to see exactly where I was going."

"That's the way I figure it better be," Johnson replied. "It ain't that we don't trust you, but that claim's about all we've got in the world, and we haven't even filed on it yet. And you've already said you won't make a deal till you've seen the claim. Now, if we close a deal when you see what we've got, that's all well and good. But if we don't—"

"I understand the way you feel about protecting the location of your claim, Mr. Johnson," Jessie broke in. "And I can't say I blame you."

"Then you'll ride out there—well, just the same as if you had on a blindfold, being in the wagon the way we'd fix it up."

Jessie waited for a moment before replying. Then she said, "I don't imagine I'd be very comfortable, but I'll have to agree that your scheme would solve our problem."

"If it's agreeable to you, then, let's work it out that way," Johnson suggested.

Ki had listened silently while Johnson outlined his idea. Now he asked, "I suppose there'd be room for me in the wagon?"

"I don't see why not," Johnson replied. "But you'll still have to make the last leg in the wagon, covered up so you can't see anything."

"Then let's leave it as you've suggested," Jessie said. "Just tell us where and when we can meet in—oh, say ten days, or better still, two weeks from today."

"Well, about the only way to go is to take that new spur the Southern Pacific's pushing across the bottom of Arizona Territory," Johnson said. "Railhead's at Casa Grande. I don't imagine there'll be rails past it for quite a while. From Casa Grande there's a stagecoach line on west. Ride the stage to Gila Bend, and that's where we'll meet you."

"Are you sure we can rent horses at the place you said, Casa Grande?" Ki asked.

"Oh, sure," Tek said. "It ain't a bad little town. It's got a livery stable and a rooming house with a dining room, and a store and a saloon."

"Then let's consider it settled," Jessie said briskly. "Ki and I will be there, just as we've outlined. Now, unless you gentlemen are in a hurry to get back, you're welcome to stay on at the Circle Star as long as you like."

"Oh, we'll need to hurry on, Miss Starbuck," Johnson told her. "Matter of fact, if there's a westbound evening train we can take, I'd like mighty well to be on it."

"There'll be one through about four this afternoon," Ki volunteered. "I'll see that you have horses to take you to the station. Just leave them there; the stationmaster will keep them in one of his pens until one of the Circle Star hands can pick them up."

"Its been a while since we've had to make part of a trip in a stagecoach, Ki," Jessie said as she shifted position, trying to find a yielding spot in the threadbare upholstery that covered the sagging seat of the lurching coach. "I'd almost forgotten how uncomfortable they can be."

"I'd prefer the train, myself," Ki agreed. "But we're lucky to be the only passengers who changed from the train to this coach at Casa Grande. Think what these seats would be like if the stage were crowded and we couldn't shift around now and then."

Jessie leaned forward to peer out the glassed upper section of the stagecoach door. She gazed across the vast expanse of deep yellow sand through which the stagecoach was now traveling. Its level monotony was broken only by a few low-lying rock outcrops and a few scattered stalks of cylindrical saguaro cactus. The small portion of the road which she could see was nothing more than a pair of twin threads that stretched to the level horizon.

"How much farther do you think we have to go?" she asked.

"My guess wouldn't be worth much, Jessie. I've never been through this particular part of Arizona Territory before."

"This is the third day we've been on this coach," Jessie said thoughtfully. "And unless I've miscounted, we've gone through five little towns. Surely it won't be too long before we get to the next one."

"Probably not," Ki agreed. "And it might even be the place where we're headed." He leaned toward the coach door, a half-door really, with its upper half a glassless window. He surveyed the terrain ahead for a moment before settling back into the seat and went on, "It might be wise to catch hold of the grab-strap, Jessie. There's some more rough country ahead. We're coming to another one of those rock outcrops, and this one stretches farther than I can see."

"After the bouncing we've already taken, I hope this one doesn't last a half-hour, the way the last one did," she commented as she reached up to close her hand around the loop of wide leather that hung from the side of the coach just inside the door. "My jaw's still aching from the jarring we've had."

Within the next few minutes the coach slowed, then it began to sway and creak as its big rear wheels grated on rock instead of sand. The going got rougher as they progressed and the top-heavy vehicle swayed and creaked, even though the driver had slowed the coach-horses to a walk.

In spite of the slow-down they'd covered several more miles when the high-pitched bark of a shot cut the air, then another. Ki leaned forward to look out the door opening. He saw two men on horseback, ten or a dozen yards from the stage. Both had bandannas wrapped around their faces; all that was visible of their features was their eyes under their wide pulled-down hatbrims. Both carried rifles and had cartridge bandoliers across their chests.

"Stage robbers!" Ki exclaimed as he pulled lightning-like away from the window opening.

Jessie had her rifle out and Ki was slipping a *shuriken* from its wrist-sheath when the third rifle-shot sounded above the coach's creaking.

Ki leaned forward just far enough to be able to peer through the door opening. He ducked back involuntarily when the body of the stage driver thudded against the body of the coach in its slide to the ground.

When the horses no longer felt the driver's restraining hands on the reins, they began moving faster, and the stagecoach started swaying wildly.

"Get on the floor, Jessie!" Ki called over his shoulder.

His answer was the sharp crack of Jessie's Winchester. She was kneeling on the coach floor now, her rifle shouldered.

"I missed!" she snapped angrily, bringing up the rifle's muzzle again and dropping her cheek to its stock while she sought to get the bandits in her sights again.

Ki realized instantly that even if Jessie had heard his call, she was in no mood to pay attention to it. Her total interest was concentrated on aiming her rifle, and she was beginning to shift the angle of the weapon's aim.

Ki turned back to the door opening on his side of the stagecoach. A rider was just coming into sight. Ki could not see him fully, only a slit of skin and the glint of light reflected from the outlaw's eyes and the glistening blue steel of the revolver he was holding at eye level, waiting for another target.

Ki followed the man's advance with his eyes, and when he could see him clearly wasted no time in sending his *shuriken* flashing through the air. He watched the low arc of the blade and saw it slice through the crown of the bandit's hat and bury its sharp points in his skull.

Jessie's rifle cracked again, but Ki did not take his eyes off the outlaw who'd been his target. The man was swaying in his saddle now. Suddenly his arms went slack, his revolver fell from one hand, and the reins pulled away from the other. For a moment longer he kept himself in the saddle, then he toppled to the ground and lay motionless.

Ki suddenly became aware that Jessie's rifle shot had not brought a reply from the gun of the man who'd drawn her fire. Ki glanced around. She was still holding her rifle shouldered, while the outlaw's body was sliding from the horse.

"Did you get one?" she asked Ki.

"Yes. You dropped another one before that one who just fell off his horse, didn't you?"

"Yes," she replied. "And I didn't see any more. Did you?"

"No. But they'd be in back of us now. And I've got to get up to the seat and rein in the horses!" Ki said. "I think we got all of the outlaws, but you watch and cover me!"

Without waiting for Jessie to reply, Ki leaned as far out the window as he could and twisted his torso until he could reach up and get a firm grip on the iron bar of the luggage rack that ran around the top of the vehicle. Then he began levering himself out of the stagecoach.

★

Chapter 6

No more shots sounded while Ki hauled himself to the top of the bouncing, swaying vehicle. He crouched on his hands and knees for a moment while he looked back. Three riderless horses were standing motionless on the barren rock-strewn ground, tossing their heads and flicking their tails.

On the baked earth the bodies of three men who'd been in the animals' saddles were sprawled some little distance away from the horses. A quick glance told Ki that all three of the men in the group were lying motionless, their twisted postures the mark of death. A fourth body, equally still, lay huddled on the ground between the coach and the three horses. Though Ki could not see the dead man's face, the clothing told him that it was the body of the stage driver.

Scrabbling across the top of the lurching stagecoach, Ki lowered himself into the high driver's seat and bent forward to grasp the slack reins. The shooting had excited the animals, and they had their bits in their teeth, but had not yet gained enough speed to be uncontrollable. Ki sawed at the reins until he brought the team to a halt, then he looped the reins tightly around the seat-rail and dropped to the ground.

"They got the driver with their first shots," Ki said as he reached the stagecoach door and opened it for Jessie. While she was stepping to the ground he went on, "And luck, along with your good shooting, kept us from getting a scratch."

"We were both lucky," Jessie replied as she took the long step to the ground. She looked at the bodies of the three outlaws lying on the hard sunbaked soil, and that of the driver, huddled on the hard expanse of baked earth between them and the bandits. "But the ugly little job we've got to do now, burying these outlaws and the driver, is going to make us awfully late getting to Gila Bend."

"I imagine whoever's supposed to meet us there will still be waiting," Ki said. "And we won't be too badly delayed if we don't take time to dig graves."

"We can't just ride away and leave these bodies for the buzzards and wild animals, Ki! And in this rocky ground, it'll take us forever to dig graves for them."

"That's not what I meant. This isn't any place to dig graves, Jessie, there are more rock outcrops than there is dirt," Ki went on. "Let's just load them in the coach. You and I can squeeze into the driver's seat for the rest of the way."

"That'll save a lot of time," Jessie agreed. "And the sooner we get them into the stage, the sooner we can start moving again. We can't be too far from Gila Bend by now, and I'm sure we'd both rather be there than here."

• • •

Working like the team they'd become during hours spent together on the Circle Star and in perilous situations in many encounters during the years when they were battling the cartel, Jessie and Ki wasted little time in talk. They moved with quick efficiency, tackling the unpleasant job of carrying the dead men to the stagecoach one by one and arranging their limp forms inside it. After loading the outlaws' weapons in the possum-belly that dangled below the stage, they fastened the bridles of the outlaws' horses to the back of the vehicle and climbed up to the driver's high seat.

Ki took the reins and slapped them across the backs of the stage horses, and the rested animals moved forward. The road now somehow seemed rougher than ever. It veered sharply around rock outcrops, and the load carried by the old lumbering creaking coach did not encourage speed. The clumsy swaying stagecoach had obviously been used long and hard, by drivers who were careless about such details as greasing its axle-joints and keeping its iron tires in good shape.

Still, they made steady progress over the rough road while the sun dropped lower in the western sky. As was usual when they were making a journey together in a cart or wagon, Jessie and Ki took turns at the reins. Jessie was holding the leathers when the sound of something she could not quite identify caught her attention. She glanced around to find its source. As she was turning her head she saw a flicker of movement at the roadside close to the stagecoach. She turned her eyes downward, examining the ground, thinking that the pinging might be caused by some new formation of soil or rocks in the twin ruts of the roadbed. Then she blinked with surprise when she saw a large hoop rolling in an erratic wobble only a few inches from the side of the coach.

"Ki!" she exclaimed. "There's something rolling out—"

Ki's raised voice interrupted her when he said, "Jessie! We've lost a tire! We'd better pull up fast or we might lose the wheel as well!"

Jessie was already sawing at the reins. The horses reared in protest as the bits dug into their jaws, and the stagecoach stopped. In the few minutes that had passed, the hoop had rolled on for a short distance ahead of the coach before its wobble grew more and more erratic and it toppled to the baked ground.

"We can't lose that tire!" Ki said. "Hold the horses for a minute, Jessie. I'll go get it."

Leaping from the high seat of the stagecoach, Ki flexed his knees to ease the momentum of his landing and kept his balance as he hit the ground. He walked up to the wagon tire and levered it erect. The top of the unwieldy metal loop was almost as high as his chin; it was almost too big in diameter for him to span with his outspread fingers.

"It looks like we'll have to turn ourselves into blacksmiths and put this tire back on the wheel ourselves," he told Jessie as she began walking to join him after swinging out of her seat. "I'm afraid that's going to take a little doing, since we don't have the tools for the job."

"There might be some tools in the boot," Jessie suggested. She'd reached Ki's side now and bent forward to take a closer look at the wagon tire. "I know there aren't any in the possum-belly, both of us saw that when we were stuffing the outlaws' gear in it."

"There's not a tool of any kind on that coach, Jessie," Ki replied. "I looked in the boot when I was loading our gear in it before we started from Bowie, and all it had in it was the driver's valise and a pile of old rags."

"We'll just have to put the rim back on without tools, then," Jessie said. There was no hint of discouragement in her voice. "We'll find a way to get moving again, but I'll be the first to admit that it's going to take a little bit of doing."

Rolling the iron tire between them, Jessie and Ki returned to the stagecoach. Though he was sure that he'd seen no sign of a tool in the boot, Ki went to the back of the vehicle and lifted the wide flap of thick bullhide that formed the boot's cover. All that the compartment contained was the bags that he'd tossed in so casually and the heap of dirty raveling rags and the valise that the dead driver had obviously put into the compartment before they'd left Casa Grande.

After poking at the rags and finding nothing, Ki lifted the valise without any expectation of seeing anything helpful. To his pleased surprise, the valise had been resting on a large blacksmith's hammer. Picking up the hammer, Ki started back to the side of the coach.

"We've had a bit of luck," he told Jessie, who was standing beside the rimless wheel, studying it. "We do have a tool after all, but I'm not sure it's going to help us much."

"One tool's better than none at all, Ki," Jessie replied. "Now all we've got to do is figure out a way to lift the wheel off the ground so that we can get the tire back on."

"And keep it on until we get to Gila Bend," Ki reminded her. "That's going to be the trick."

"Let's solve one problem at a time," Jessie suggested. "Do you think if we unloaded the stage, the two of us might be able to lift it?"

"No. But we'd be fools not to try."

They moved to the rimless wheel and found handholds on its spokes. Then Jessie counted to three, and they both strained as they tried to raise the stagecoach, but it did not budge.

"Maybe if we unloaded it—" Jessie began.

Ki shook his head. "It'll take a lever of some kind to get this stagecoach lifted even an inch or two off the ground."

"Do you think we can get the rim back on the wheel even if we can lift it?"

"Of course," Ki assured her. "It'll be loose, and we'll still be in trouble unless we can figure out a way to keep it from coming off again."

"Yes, I know that, Ki! I've seen one or two lazy cowhands at the Circle Star try to drive a wagon with a wheel rim off, and seen the wheel come to pieces. This wheel will do the same thing unless it's got a proper rim on it."

Ki had been looking around, surveying the barren landscape thoughtfully while Jessie talked. Now he said, "The first thing we'll need is a lever that we can use to lift this side of the coach. We're lucky on one count; that grove of trees where those outlaws were hiding isn't too far back."

"Yes, I remember it," Jessie said, nodding. "There were some cedars and cottonwoods in it. Cottonwood's too brittle, but a big cedar branch will be strong enough to use as a lever."

"I'll dig my *ko-dachai* out of my luggage and go cut

one," Ki volunteered. "I've used it before when I needed to cut a limb off a tree and didn't have a saw. You rest and think while I'm doing that."

"Instead of just sitting and thinking, I'll use the time to set up a fulcrum," Jessie told him. "It won't be hard. I'll pile up a heap of stones by the wheel we need to lift. And that leaves just one more problem we'll have to solve."

"Yes, I know," Ki said. "We'll have to find a way to keep the rim on the wheel for the rest of the trip. I'm sure we both realize that we can't heat the rim to expand it and let it lock itself to the wheel when it shrinks, the way a blacksmith does. But maybe you'll get an idea while I'm cutting our lever, and I'll be trying to come up with an answer, too."

Walking to the grove of trees, Ki cudgled his brain trying to think of a way other than heat-shrinking to fit the iron rim onto the stagecoach wheel. He'd often watched the itinerant blacksmith who stopped by the Circle Star every five or six months to take care of jobs requiring a skilled metal-worker.

Ki knew how long a wait was required to heat an iron wagon tire, rotating it in the glowing red heat of a charcoal fire in a forge until the metal had expanded. He also knew that long-handled tongs were needed to turn the tire and then to lift it from the coals and fit it to the wheel, beating it into place quickly with quick sharp blows of a heavy hammer before it had time to cool and shrink as it bonded itself firmly to the wheel's perimeter.

Nails wouldn't do the job, even if we had any, Ki thought to himself as he walked. *They're soft iron; their heads would be worn smooth after a few miles over this rocky ground. We need steel, and the only steel Jessie and I have between us is my* ko-dachai *and my* shuriken. *They're both fine steel, and are—*

He stopped short, nodding his head now as he said aloud, "Of course! Brittle steel! Just what we need!"

Ki's moment of inspiration passed, but it was now firmly imbedded in his memory. He walked faster and in only a few more minutes reached the grove. Scanning the cedars quickly, he selected a long, stout low-hanging branch on one of the trees. With the razor-keen edge of his fighting-knife, he cut deep V-shaped notches where the branch joined the tree's trunk.

When he'd circled the joint, Ki made a second series of cuts to deepen and widen the notches. Then he closed his strong hands over the branch and alternated pulling it down and lifting it up until it cracked and gave way and broke off at the cutline. Shaving the twigs off the branch as he walked, Ki went back to where Jessie was waiting beside the stagecoach.

"That certainly ought to be strong enough and long enough," Jessie nodded when Ki laid the branch beside the stagecoach. "And we'll only have to lift it an inch or so, just high enough to slip the rim onto the wheel. But what about keeping it in place? If it's not wedged firmly, it'll come right off again."

"I've got the answer, " Ki told her. "Or at least, I think I have. I brought enough *shuriken* to have some spares. We'll do a little experimenting and see if I'm right."

"But what about tools?" Jessie frowned. "That hammer's the only thing we've got."

"If I'm right, it's the only thing we'll need," Ki told her. "Let's take a look at those rocks."

While he'd been busy with the cedar branch, Jessie had dragged a half-dozen sizable rocks up to the coach. Ki looked at a half-dozen before finding one that was flat enough and big enough to suit him. He put it beside the wheel and searched among the stones until he found another suitable one. Then he turned to Jessie and smiled when he saw her puzzled frown.

"We have an anvil and a hammer now," Ki said. He was taking a *shuriken* from the circular pouch strapped to his forearm as he spoke. "Let's become metalsmiths for a moment."

"I'm afraid you've lost me," Jessie said. "How can we use those rocks and your *shuriken* to keep that rim on the stagecoach wheel?"

"We may not be able to," Ki told her. "But it's worth a try. What I'm thinking of doing is using the points from one of my *shuriken* to hold the rim in place."

"But how?" Jessie repeated.

"You'll see how while we're working," Ki told her. "You do have your riding gloves in your bag, don't you?"

"I've got them right here in my pocket," Jessie said. "Do you mind telling me why you need them?"

"I don't need them, but you do," Ki replied. He held up the *shuriken* as he went on: "The steel in these is brittle, Jessie. If you're holding the blade at right angles to the edge of that flat rock, I'm gambling that I can hit the points with enough force to snap them off. Then we can drive the points into the wood at a half-dozen places to hold the rim in place."

"Won't they pop out when we start moving?"

"That's something we won't find out until we've gone a little way. I'm hoping they'll just cut into the ground and that enough of them will stay in place as long as it takes for us to get to Gila Bend."

"They just may, at that," Jessie said, nodding. A thoughtful frown grew on her face as she spoke. "But if we lose a few, we can stop and put others in to replace them." As she spoke Jessie was taking her gloves from her pocket. She went on: "All right, Ki. Let's get started trying your scheme. You be the village blacksmith, and I'll be your apprentice."

Ki had taken a *shuriken* from his arm-case while Jessie was pulling her gloves on. He selected a stone with a flat surface and a sharp edge and placed the *shuriken* on it, one of the blade's points protruding beyond the edge of his improvised anvil. Picking through the smaller stones, he found one shaped like an apothecary's pestle.

Jessie kneeled and pressed on the *shuriken* with the heels of both hands, leaning forward to hold it firmly. Ki studied the blade and the stone for a moment, then brought his improvised hammer down with all his considerable strength. The hammer-stone hit its mark with a sharp metallic *thwack,* and the point which had been Ki's target dropped to the ground.

Ki expelled the breath he'd been holding, then said, "You know, I really wasn't sure that our idea was going to work. Turn the blade to the next point, Jessie. Let's get enough of them broken off to go around that wheel, then we'll see how the rest of our scheme works out."

For the next half-hour Jessie and Ki used their improvised hammer and anvil to break the triangular points off two of his *shuriken,* then Ki laid aside his hammer stone. Jessie had picked up each point as it was broken from the blade, and she gathered them up, then stood beside Ki, spreading the metal triangles out on her upturned palm.

"We've got more than enough, I'd say," she told him. "We can space them out along the wheel as we drive them in. The only way of finding out whether this idea's going to work is to try it, and I'd say the sooner we find out, the better."

For another busy half-hour she and Ki hammered the pointed bits of steel into the stagecoach wheel, spacing them on each side of the loose iron tire, moving the coach ahead now and then to reach the wheel's entire circumference. At last they stepped back to inspect their work.

"It certainly doesn't look fancy, but I don't think we ever expected it to," Jessie said. "The big question is, will it work?"

"We'll know soon enough," Ki told her. "One thing that I can see right now is that we'll have to be sure to keep the stage where the ground's soft. I've got an idea that those points will pop out if we try to take the stage across any rocky places."

Fresh after their long rest, the stagecoach horses gave Ki's muscular arms very little rest while he wrestled the reins to keep them from going too fast after they started out.

Both he and Jessie sat on the edge of the high seat, looking alternately at the terrain ahead or their horses on lead ropes behind the slowly moving vehicle, or down at the wheels to check on the condition of their jerry-built repair job as the crippled wheel rotated slowly, the edges of the *shuriken* points cutting a strange track in the dry soil as the stagecoach moved steadily ahead.

Now and then one of the points became loose and dropped off the wheel, but it was the job of only a minute or so to hammer in a replacement. In spite of these stops they made good time while the sun dropped steadily toward the western horizon.

There was very little change in the character of the country they were crossing. Greenery was scarce, the dun-colored hue of sandy earth predominated, and aside from an occasional brownish-red rock outdrop the only color came from the light olive-green of a seemingly endless number of cactus clumps. The plants ranged from the head-high twisted and bent arms of a stand of cholla, studded with spines instead of leaves, to the small plump clumps of barrel cacti which looked like nothing more than thorn-encrusted bowling balls.

"I'll take the grassy Circle Star range over this kind of country any day, Ki," Jessie remarked as she turned her eyes away from the sameness of the landscape. "There's not enough grass hereabouts to feed even two or three steers, let alone a herd."

"I won't argue that with you," Ki replied, looking up from one of his frequent inspections of the jerrybuilt wheel. "But if the story those three men told us about diamonds being scattered on the surface is true, you might change your mind."

"Perhaps. But right now I'd settle for a look at anything except what we've been seeing."

"You may be getting your wish granted before too long," Ki told her. He gestured ahead. "Those straight lines that've just come in sight look to me like houses and buildings instead of hills and low spots in this desert."

Jessie followed Ki's pointing finger with her eyes. Against the pinkish hue which the western sky was beginning to take on with the approach of sunset, she could see the cluster of level horizontal lines that could mean only rooftops.

"I think you're right," she replied. "And it's the first sign of civilization we've seen since we left Casa Grande."

Soon the square blocks of buildings rose to break the level line between earth and sky.

"It must be Gila Bend," Ki told Jessie. "There's not another town shown on the map anywhere around here, and that pile of tumbled-down adobe bricks must be the old Indian pueblo that the man they call Tek told us to look for."

"Oh, it's where we're headed, all right," Jessie agreed. "We'll not only get rid of this ghastly load of bodies here, Ki. I'm going to insist on staying here for a day or two of rest before we start out for the diamond fields, as curious as I am to see whether they really exist or whether we've come all this way on a harum-scarum wild-goose chase."

★

Chapter 7

Jessie and Ki rode toward Gila Bend trying to shield their faces from the setting sun. The glare from above and the heat waves rising from the baked grayish-yellow soil forced them to keep their eyes slitted, and to concentrate on following the faint trace the road had become. Neither the shod hooves of horses nor the iron tires of wagon wheels made a lasting impression on the crusted soil.

By the time they'd gotten near enough to distinguish any of the individual structures in the little clump of buildings, the sun had dropped below the crests of a low spur of mountains that rose beyond the town. However, the cloudless sky remained bright, and as the distance lessened to a mile or so, they could not only make out the town's buildings but could catch an occasional glint of the sky's reflection from the surface of the river that flowed beyond it.

Looking down into the V formed by the shallow river valley, they quickly understood why the man who'd mentioned Gila Bend had described it as "not such a much" of a town. From what they could see in the final clear light of the declining day, the community was one street long and two streets wide. The long street was the road that they were following into the settlement. The two other streets crossed the road and extended beyond it for not much more than a quarter of a mile in each side.

When they drew closer, Jessie and Ki could see that even the main thoroughfare was short; the town began and ended abruptly, a brief interruption of the trackless uninhabited desert. There was still enough daylight for them to glimpse the curving course of the Gila River beyond the town, where a sharp half-loop at the base of a spur of hills shooting out from the higher peaks beyond that had forced the riverbed into the abrupt change of course and had given the town its name.

On the stream's bank they saw the jagged lines of partly fallen walls of adobe brick beside the riverbank. Because of the disance they could make out little of the details of the age-ruined structure, but it was obvious even so far away that the ruins were what remained of an ancient Indian pueblo.

On reaching the town's outskirts Jessie and Ki began looking for some kind of official building, but none was evident. There were signs on the half-dozen stores that lined the main street, but only two of these were of any interest to them. Jessie gave a sigh of relief when she saw the sign that bore the legend HOTEL, and on the street at right angles to the hotel and just behind it a rambling barnlike structure had an even larger sign: LIVERY STABLE.

"It'll be convenient to have them so close together," Jessie told Ki, gesturing toward the signs as the stagecoach rolled down the town's main street. "Now all we need to do is to find a sheriff or constable or whoever enforces the law here. We'll turn the stagecoach and the bodies over to him and check into the hotel. If we're lucky it'll have a bath of some kind, and real beds to sleep in."

"A bed will feel good," Ki agreed. "And a bath will be even better. But why don't you just go to the hotel and register for both of us, Jessie? Unless those diamond-peddlers have already gotten here, we don't have anything to do except turn this stagecoach over to whoever's responsible for it, and I can take care of that while you're getting settled in."

"Don't you suppose the sheriff or constable will want to know why we're bringing in four dead bodies?"

"Of course, but I can explain all that to him. If he wants to ask you anything, he can come to the hotel. Right now I'm thinking about just turning the stagecoach over to whoever's in charge of it and have him notify the authorities."

"That might be the best way," Jessie agreed. "I'll take your suggestion, Ki. After you've delivered the coach, you can freshen up, and we'll see if we can't find a restaurant where we can get a meal that's been cooked on a stove instead of a campfire, or eaten right out of an airtight because we couldn't find enough wood for a fire."

"I'll pull up here, then," Ki said, reining in at the entrance to the hotel. "Then, after I've carried our gear in, I'll take the stagecoach around the corner to the livery and get it off our hands."

Ki was reining up in front of the hotel as he spoke. Jessie went in while he took their gear out of the possum belly, then followed her inside. Ki reached the hotel desk in time to hear the clerk behind it say to Jessie, "Well, seeing as how it's you, Miss Starbuck, I'll bend our rules and let your servant stay here."

“Ki is not my servant!” Jessie said coldly. “He’s both my trusted assistant and my friend. Please remember that.”

“I ain’t likely to forget it, ma’am. Now, if you’ll just sign the register, I’ll see your gear gets upstairs just as soon as the porter finishes what he’s doing.”

“Thank you,” Jessie said. Her voice was still icy. “And please tell the porter we’ll both want hot baths before dinner.”

“Yes, ma’am, Miss Starbuck, I’ll see to it,” the man said, nodding. “And if there’s anything else you need—”

“I’ll let you know,” Jessie replied. She turned to Ki and went on: “Johnson and his friends haven’t gotten here yet.” She handed Ki a crumpled telegraph flimsy. “But as you can see, we haven’t been forgotten. This was waiting for us.”

Ki unfolded the telegraph flimsy. It was addressed simply to “Miss Jessica Starbuck, in care of hotel, Gila Bend, Arizona Ter.” Ki read: “Unavoidably delayed starting. Please wait. Will be only a few days late.” The message was signed by Jack Johnson.

“I notice they don’t give any reason for being late,” Ki remarked as he handed the message back to Jessie. “But I’m sure they’ll have some good reason.”

“Oh, of course. And I don’t really mind, Ki,” Jessie replied. “It’s been a hard trip, and we’ll enjoy resting for a day or two before we go with them to their diamond field.”

“I’ll go and get the stagecoach off our hands, then,” Ki told her.

Jessie nodded, saying, “And as soon as we’ve gotten rid of our travel dust, we’ll have dinner and start resting.”

• • •

"Bodies!" the liveryman exclaimed when Ki had told him of the stagecoach's unpleasant contents. "I'm just the stagecoach company's agent! I'll take care of the passengers, like I'm supposed to, but what the living hell you expect me to do with dead men?"

"Notify your sheriff or town marshal, or whoever's responsible for law enforcement here, to begin with," Ki replied. "I suppose you'll know who he is. And I'd imagine you'll want to notify the stagecoach company, or have him do it for you."

"I'll take care of the stage and the driver," the liveryman said. His voice was calmer now. "Like you say, that's my job. But the town marshal's office is just a step down the street, so you kite on down there and tell him about the ones you said was outlaws. And tell him I'll thank him to come take their bodies off my hands quick as he can!"

Ki walked the short distance to the Gila Bend marshal's office and stood in the open doorway for a moment before stepping inside. A burly man was sitting in front of a battered rolltop desk. His broad-brimmed hat was pushed back on his head, and he was studying the sheaf of "WANTED" notices that he was shuffling from one hand to the other. He looked up when Ki's shadow blocked the light from the doorway.

"You want something?" he asked.

"I have some"—Ki paused for a moment while he chose the correct words, then went on—"some bodies that I need to turn over to you."

"Bodies? You talking about dead men now, I take it?" the lawman frowned.

Ki nodded. "Dead outlaws. Two of them. They murdered a stagecoach driver while they were trying to hold up the stage from Casa Grande." Ki paused, but the questions he'd expected did not follow. He went on: "I am here with Miss Jessica Starbuck. We were passengers on the stage. When the outlaws tried to stop the stage, we fought them off, but they'd already killed the driver."

"That'd be Seth Morris?" The marshal frowned.

"I don't know what his name was," Ki replied. "But his body is also in the stagecoach. The man at the livery said he'd see to burying him, but he's anxious to get rid of the others."

"Looks to me like I better step along with you and see what all this is about," the marshal said. He got to his feet and tossed the circulars on the desk. "Come along—I didn't get your name?"

"Ki."

"Ki what? And from where?"

"Just Ki, marshal, I work for Miss Starbuck. We came here from Texas on business. Miss Starbuck owns a large ranch, the Circle Star, in west Texas."

"Well, now," the marshal said, frowning, "that's a hell of a yarn you been spinning me, and I still ain't sure how what you're saying all comes together. But let's go on over to the livery. I'm sorta curious to find out just what this is all about."

"And the marshal was finally satisfied with your story?" Jessie asked Ki.

They were sitting at one of the small tables in the hotel's restaurant. Jessie and Ki were the only occupants of the room. Their supper, steak and potatoes, had been tasty enough, though Jessie had frowned in distaste of the soiled and smeared apron of the waiter who'd served them.

"I suppose he was," Ki said. "He knew who the dead outlaws were. It seems they've been very active in this vicinity for the past several months. I tried to answer all his questions, and he seemed to accept what I told him. But he might come and talk to you later, perhaps tomorrow."

Jessie nodded. Then she said, "Since we saw that big ruin of the old Indian pueblo yesterday, I've been wondering about it, Ki. It seems that we'll have at least a day or two of waiting, and instead of doing nothing in this little place that's just like so many we've seen before, suppose we ride out tomorrow and take a close look at those ruins. Or had you rather just stay here at the hotel and rest?"

"I think I'd prefer to keep busy, Jessie," Ki replied. "It's a little hard to come to a sudden stop after we've been so busy, and I'm a bit curious about those ruins myself."

"That's what we'll do, then," she nodded. "Sleep late, have an early lunch, and spend the afternoon looking at ruins. It'll be just enough activity to keep us from getting stiff, and restful enough so that we won't be too tired to finish our trip with the diamond swindlers."

"You seem to be sure they're crooks, Jessie. I think so, too, of course, but I can't put my finger on anything they said or did that gave me the idea."

"Neither could I, as improbable as their story is. But I try not to close my mind to any kind of discoveries, Ki. I just think of James Marshall finding gold at Sutter's Mill back in 1848, and remind myself that even the most unlikely things are very often possible."

Rested after sleeping until almost noon, Jessie and Ki had a combined breakfast and lunch, enjoyed a brief siesta and set out for the ruins of the ancient pueblo in the early afternoon. In the tricky sunlight of the desert afternoon the ruins of the old Indian settlement beside the river looked closer than they really were. Almost an hour passed before Jessie and Ki reined in beside the sprawling ruins of the long-abandoned pueblo and sat staring at them.

"There must have been a lot of people living here when this place was new," Jessie observed. "Why, it covers almost as much ground as the town back there does."

"I don't suppose anybody knows how many today," Ki said. "And maybe nobody even knows who the people were who built it or how many of them there were or when they lived here or why they left or when."

"No, but it was certainly a long time ago," Jessie went on. "Hundreds of years, I'm sure. I think I'll go walk around them for a little while, Ki. In a deserted spot like this, this place wouldn't have many visitors. Even after all these years there might be a few things left in them, maybe some pieces of pottery or a scrap of a blanket. You know how this desert air preserves things. We just might find something that would be interesting to look at."

"Fine," Ki agreed. "I've done enough riding for a while. I'll be glad to get the kinks out of my legs."

Dropping the reins of the livery horses to the ground so the animals would stand, Jessie and Ki walked up to the walls of the ancient pueblo. Even after all the years since it had been abandoned, the walls of adobe bricks were in good shape in spite of their lack of roofs. Most of the vigas, the rafters made from sturdy tree saplings which had supported the roofs of the rooms, were still in place, though the roof coverings themselves had long since vanished. So had the window casings and doors and the boards which had framed them.

Jessie wandered into one of the door openings, and Ki chose another to enter. He moved slowly from room to room. The layout of the old building indicated that the rooms were all interconnected, for there was no sign of a hallway.

Ki moved in the opposite direction from the one Jessie had chosen to explore. It was obvious that the Indians who'd built and then abandoned the pueblo so many years ago had either taken everything of value with them when they moved, or that souvenir-hunters had cleaned out the place during the years since its builders had departed. There were a few shards of plates and water pots or other pottery vessels on the floors of some of the rooms, but these were only bits and pieces.

Ki had covered three or four rooms, moving deeper and deeper into the ruins, when he first heard the alien sounds. He paid little attention to the first faint noises, sure that Jessie was making them in her own explorations. Then, from somewhere close at hand, he heard the unmistakable low rumbling snarls and angry hisses that could only have come from the throat of a panther.

Then over the snarls and throaty growls he heard a woman's voice pleading, "Please, big cat, go away! I haven't done anything to you! All I want to do is get down from here and leave you alone! Go on, now! Go away!"

At any other time Ki might have questioned the logic of a person trying to persuade an animal with words, but the woman's voice told him that she was approaching the brink of panic. He hurried across the room in the direction from which the sounds were coming and stopped short in the doorway when he saw the tableau in the room beyond.

In the far corner of the room a young woman was pressing her back into the angle made by the joining walls. Her face was a study in terror, eyes wide, mouth open, and her extended arms were pressing hard against the walls. On the floor near the center of the room a panther was crouched facing her. The big yellow cat held its belly to the ground and its tail was sweeping the floor, moving slowly in an arc that raised a small cloud of dust each time it moved.

Although the big cat did not turn to look at Ki, it was obvious that the animal had heard him approaching or had scented his presence when Ki came into the room. The volume of its angry threatening growls and snarls rose, and now they poured from its throat in an almost constant stream and in a higher pitch than before. The girl pressed into the corner had not yet seen Ki, for her eyes were fixed on the hissing, snarling cat.

Ki did not dare to speak and warn the young woman to remain motionless, but his hands moved with the swift precision of long experience. He brought them together, and his right hand found the case strapped to his left forearm in which he carried his *shuriken*. His fingers working with the speed and precision of practice as well as long use, he slid two of the razor-sharp steel throwing-blades from the leather carrying case.

Though Ki's movements were slight and he did his best to work silently, the panther either heard him or had caught Ki's alien scent. A ripple passed over the big cat's tawny skin and its menacing snarls grew even louder.

Suddenly, without any sort of warning hint, the puma whirled to face Ki. Its fearsome yellowed fangs bared in the frame of its gaping jaws, Ki saw the sinewy muscles of its hind legs bunch below its tawny skin and its tail shot up as it launched itself through the air in a spring intended to end on Ki's shoulders.

Ki's speed and skill were greater than the puma's. He had his *shuriken* ready to launch by the time the feral cat had twirled to face him, and he judged its path through the air in the tiny fraction of a second that the puma was sailing toward him.

As the big feral cat rose in its leaping attack, Ki sent a *shuriken* twirling to intercept it. The steel blade sliced into one of the puma's eyes as Ki dropped to the floor and rolled toward the airborne animal. The puma yowled as it brought up its forepaws while still in midair to claw at the biting blade.

Ki bunched himself into a ball and rolled under the puma while it was still in midair. He brought himself to his knees, the second *shuriken* in his throwing hand. The puma landed at the base of the wall where Ki had been standing. It was still pawing with its forefeet at the imbedded throwing-blade and the big cat did not land on all-fours with its usual grace, but fell with a thud in a sprawling heap.

Ki was ready before the cat recovered from its fall. As the puma found its balance and got all four feet on the floor, Ki sent his second *shuriken* in its whirling flight. His target had been the puma's neck, but the animal was moving so swiftly in its recovery from the fall that the blade went wide of its mark and buried itself in the rippling shoulder muscle just above the big cat's foreleg.

Its instinct to survive replaced the puma's intention to attack. It yowled in defeat as it whirled away from the black apparition that had inflicted such pain on it, and in spite of its wounded shoulder muscle the animal leaped through the doorway beside it and disappeared.

Carrying a *shuriken* in his hand, Ki stepped to the door quickly. The puma was still within range of his blade, but it was in full retreat now, covering the ground in leaps. Ki stood watching while the big animal's limping gait took it out of range of his throws and out of sight behind a hump in the sandy soil.

Ki turned back to the girl cowering into the corner of the room. She had not moved during the few moments that had passed since Ki first came through the doorway. Her eyes were wide, her mouth open, an expression of shocked disbelief on her face.

"You have nothing more to worry about now," Ki told her. His voice was low and gently soothing. "The big cat will not be back, and I will not harm you."

"Who—who are you?" the girl asked, finding her voice at last.

"My name is Ki. I came here with Miss Starbuck, the lady whom I serve. When I heard the puma's growls, and your voice, I came to see what was happening."

"And you got here just in time," the girl said. "I don't want to think about what would've happened to me if you hadn't shown up when you did."

"Then don't think about it. I was only glad—" Ki broke off as Jessie's voice sounded from the doorway.

"Ki!" she said. "What—" She saw the girl for the first time and stopped short for a moment, then asked, "Would one of you please tell me just what's been going on?"

Chapter 8

"It's very simple, Jessie," Ki said. "This young lady was backed into that corner by a mountain lion. I heard it growling and came to see what was happening. It turned to attack me, and I drove it off with a couple of *shuriken*."

"I heard it growling and yowling," Jessie said. "That's what brought me to investigate." Turning to the girl, who was still pressed into her sheltering corner, she went on: "I'm Jessica Starbuck. Ki and I are in Gila Bend on business. I suppose you live here?"

"Yes. My name's Callie Mae Stafford. I work in—" She hesitated for a split-second, then went on, her voice a bit defiant: "I work in the Big Strike Saloon. You likely don't know about it, being strangers in town. It's down at the end of Main Street."

Jessie's expression did not change, nor did the tone of her voice as she went on: "Well, Miss Stafford, I've no idea what brought you out to these ruins, but from what's happened—"

"I come out every now and then," Callie Mae broke

in. "You know, Miss Starbuck, a girl gets sorta tired smelling sour beer and whiskey that's spilled on the floor and having the customers yelling at her night after night. At least it's quiet, and I can get a breath of fresh air out here. And I like to walk through the rooms and wonder about what this place used to be like, with the Indians living in it and all."

"I see," Jessie said, nodding. "But unless you have some good reason to keep you here, it might be a good idea for you to ride back to town with Ki and me. That puma might return, or there might be another one prowling around."

"I'll be real glad to have company going back," Callie Mae answered. "My horse is out in back of the building here. It ain't that I'm all that much afraid, but I sure wouldn't want to be here by myself if that mountain lion shows up again."

They talked little on the ride back to town. When they got to the hotel, Jessie and Ki reined in at the corner before turning their horses toward the livery stable, and Callie Mae was quick to pull up her mount as well.

She said, "I sure do thank you for saving me from that mountain lion, Ki. And you, too, Miss Starbuck."

"Give Ki full credit; I didn't come in until he'd run the beast off," Jessie said with a smile. "But when you go out to those ruins again, you'd better take a rifle or a pistol. There might be another mountain lion in the neighborhood."

"Oh, shucks, Miss Starbuck, I've been out there a lot of times and never seen one of those critters until today. But I'll do what you said and take a gun next time." Turning to Ki, she went on: "And I thank you special,

Ki. If you get thirsty for a drink, you know where to find it, and I'll see you get served on the house."

"I'll remember," Ki said with a nod. "We may be in town a few days, depending on when the men we're waiting for get here."

"I'll bid you good-bye, now," Callie said, toeing her horse into motion. Over her shoulder she added, "Remember, if either one of you needs anything, being strangers here and all, just come to me and I'll help you all I can."

"She seems a cut above most of the saloon girls I've run into," Jessie commented as she and Ki guided their horses toward the livery stable. "And from the little I saw, you certainly saved her from a bad mauling."

"I just did what was necessary," Ki said with a shrug as they dismounted. The stableman had seen them ride in and was heading toward them. Before they could take more than a step toward the hotel, he raised his voice and called.

"Miss Starbuck!" He waited until Jessie turned to face him and went on: "There was three men come in a little while ago, and they asked about whether you was here or not. I told 'em you was before I stopped to think that you might not've wanted anybody to know. Hope I didn't do nothing wrong."

"You didn't," Jessie assured him. "We've been expecting them, but weren't sure when they'd ride in."

"Well, they'll be waiting for you inside, I imagine," the liveryman said. "I'm sure glad I didn't make no mistake."

As Jessie and Ki left the liveryman and started toward the hotel, she said, "It seems that our friends finished whatever business delayed them and got here sooner than they'd expected to when they sent their telegram."

"Either they left earlier or the telegram was delayed," Ki said. "Or it may just be that we're not as far from their so-called diamond fields as we'd thought."

Jessie frowned. "That hadn't occurred to me, Ki. But you just might be right. Whatever's the reason for them getting here earlier than we'd expected, it'll be interesting to find out what they have to say now."

Their discovery of the reason for the diamond swindlers unexpectedly early arrival was not long delayed. The moment that Jessie and Ki entered the hotel, they saw both Jack Johnson and Tek Powell start across the lobby to greet them. A third man was with them.

"We just happened to be looking out the window and saw you riding into the livery stable, Miss Starbuck," Johnson said. "I'm sorry we had to delay our meeting, but there was a bit more to take care of at our claim than we'd expected."

"It's not at all important," Jessie replied. "Ki and I just got here yesterday."

"I'm glad to hear that we haven't inconvenienced you," Johnson went on. "And before I give you any of the good news that we've brought with us, I'd like to introduce our third associate, Harvey Benson. I'm sure you remember hearing us talk about him, but we generally just call him by his nickname, which is Hap."

"Of course," Jessie replied, shaking hands with the third member of the trio. "And this is Ki; you've heard of him from your associates, of course."

"Indeed I have," Benson replied. He shook hands with Jessie but did not offer his hand to Ki. Then he went on: "And Jack didn't tell you what our good news is because it's something we'd prefer to pass on when we can have a confidential talk, if there's a place where we can discuss things in private for a few minutes."

Jessie frowned, then an idea struck her. She said, "I'm afraid the rooms here are too small for a group as large as we are now, but I haven't seen a sign of there being any other guests staying here. Why don't we arrange with the hotel manager to rent us the restaurant for supper? It isn't any too large, but it'll have enough chairs for all of us, and it's as private a place as we're likely to find in a town this size."

"Excellent!" Benson agreed. He turned to Johnson and Powell and went on: "How about one of you arranging it? Miss Starbuck and Ki and I can wait here for a few minutes."

When Johnson did not volunteer at once, Tek Powell said, "I'll go ask the man. He seemed like a pretty good-hearted kind, and it ain't likely he'll say no."

Within a very few minutes Powell returned. He nodded as he reached the group and said, "We got the use of the dining room, and the help will put our supper on the table, then stay out of our way until we're through. I figure we can get our supper and business both finished in about an hour."

"That should be all the time we need," Benson agreed. "I suggest that we go in as soon as possible. We've all had a busy day, and early bedtime appeals to me."

They filed into the dining room, and for the next few moments there was a bit of confusion as the waiter dragged two tables together and spaced chairs around them.

"You can bring on our supper now," Benson told the

man. "Just put the food on the table and leave. We'll serve ourselves and leave as soon as we've got our business finished, say an hour from now."

Conversation played little part in their meal. After their long afternoon afield, Jessie and Ki were hungry, and it was obvious from the way the swindlers ate that they'd slighted food in favor of fast travel in getting to town. Dinner was finished quickly and plates pushed to the center of the table. Jessie waited patiently for several minutes, expecting one of the trio to begin, but none of them spoke. At last she decided to take matters into her own hands.

"Don't be so bashful, gentlemen," she said. "I've come this far to hear your report, so let's get to it without wasting any more time."

After a quick exchange of glances and nods between the trio, Benson shifted his chair a few inches to face Jessie and cleared his throat.

"I'm sure you understand that I'm a graduate mining engineer, Miss Starbuck," he began.

"No. Neither of your associates mentioned that to me," Jessie replied.

"Oh, I have the qualifications required to judge mineral deposits," he went on. "I didn't bring any of my diplomas or other credentials with me, of course, so—"

"We can go into your credentials later," Jessie broke in. "I'm sure you have something important to tell me, and I'm very anxious to hear what you have to say."

"Important news, Miss Starbuck," he replied. "After my associates left our find to look for someone who had capital and was interested in making a good investment, I went on with my exploration of the valley where we discovered the diamonds. And I've found that it's perhaps the richest deposit of mineral wealth ever to be found in North America."

"That's quite a broad statement, Mr. Benson," Jessie said. "Have you made an estimate of the value of these diamonds?"

"Well, now, that's a very difficult matter," Benson told her. "Almost impossible. You see, the diamonds are usually found in together in a sort of pocket, perhaps a handful of gems in one small spot. Of course, they'll be scattered sometimes, and then you'll find single stones spread over a fairly wide area."

"Yes, I can understand that," Jessie said. "But you must have some notion of the value of the entire area, this valley you and your friends speak of."

"I'd value it conservatively at—well, several million dollars, at least," Benson replied. "With a month or so to work in and make a more complete survey, I might make a more accurate judgment."

Before Benson could say anything more, Johnson spoke up: "We didn't have all the time in the world, Miss Starbuck. We wanted to be here to meet you, but all of us got sorta excited by what we found. That's why we got away later than we'd figured we would and didn't get here when we meant to."

"We talked about our situation on trip, Miss Starbuck," Benson broke in quickly. "And we've worked out a—well, not a plan, but more of an idea."

"I don't suppose you mind sharing it with me?" Jessie suggested. "After all, I've come quite a distance to meet you."

"We'd like to invite you to go back to the valley with us," Benson went on. "And see for yourself what we've found and how easy the job of taking out the diamonds will be. Then we can talk about a deal of some sort."

"I'd like to have some idea of the size investment you'd be expecting me to make," Jessie countered. "I've already seen some of the uncut stones that you say came from this deposit you've found, but I'll certainly insist on seeing the actual place where you found them."

"Oh, we've brought some new ones to show you," Johnson said, almost before Jessie had finished speaking. "And we have some good news to go along with the stones."

Without giving Jessie time to comment, Benson took a suede pouch from his coat pocket and laid it on the table between himself and Jessie. Making a ceremony of his movements, he pushed the stacked plates closer to the center of the table and picked up a napkin which he used to brush away the crumbs from the area, then untied the drawstring that was looped around the mouth of the pouch and emptied its contents on the table.

His actions reminded Jessie of the similar ritual that Powell had performed at the Circle Star, but she said nothing until Benson had freed the drawstring and upended the pouch to spill its contents on the table. In spite of herself, Jessie almost gasped when she saw the size of the largest stone. It was larger than a hen's egg, almost as big as her fist.

"That's quite a large stone you have there, Mr. Benson," Jessie remarked. "But I suppose cutting it will reduce its size quite considerably."

"Perhaps," Benson agreed. "But it would still be exceptionally large, worth hundred of thousands of dollars."

"You can't hope to find one that big every time you turn around, of course," Johnson put in. "Regardless, it'd still bring in a lot of money."

"I suppose you're sure it's a diamond?" Ki asked. "Not just a big rock?"

"I hope you're not questioning my ability to judge stones," Benson said, frowning. "My credentials—"

"Ki was just curious," Jessie broke in quickly. "But go on with what you were about to say, Mr. Benson. Seeing that large stone has certainly aroused my interest."

"Yes, of course," Benson said. "I'm sure my colleagues told you our problem, Miss Starbuck. We're not rich men, unless you count our claim to the diamond fields—"

"Which I understand hasn't been filed," Jessie interrupted. "And with your experience in mining, I'm sure you know that the first one to file on a claim gets title to it."

"Yes, of course." Benson frowned. "But you'll have to agree that we haven't made any effort to keep that a secret. My colleagues here told me that during their visit with you they made a full revelation of our situation. We haven't anything to hide, I'm sure you understand that."

"I've never questioned your intentions, Mr. Benson," Jessie replied, smiling inwardly at her double-edged answer.

"Then perhaps you'll be receptive to an offer which we're prepared to make you," Benson said. He paused expectantly.

"I couldn't say, without hearing your offer," Jessie told him calmly. "But I'm always ready to listen to an offer, for cattle or land—or diamonds."

"We've freely admitted that we're badly underfinanced," Benson went on. "Which is one of the reasons we're looking for capital. Which is why we approached you, of course."

"Of course," Jessied agreed. "Are you getting ready to make me some kind of offer now? Even before I've seen the diamond field?"

Benson seemed somewhat taken aback by Jessie's question. He took longer than usual in answering her question.

"We've discussed the possibility," he said at last. "Just as we've considered floating a public stock issue. There are also other investors we could interest in a find such as the one we've made." Benson paused, and just before he saw that Jessie was about to speak, he went on quickly, "Would you be interested in acquiring a majority of the stock in a company we would form together to exploit our diamond field, Miss Starbuck?"

Jessie did not reply at once. Her eyes flicked from Benson to Johnson to Powell. All three were waiting, hopeful expectation on their faces.

"I've always followed the pattern that my father set in his business ventures," Jessie said slowly. "He insisted on being the sole owner of any property he acquired. I'm not sure that I would want to change anything that made him so successful."

"But if you hold a clear majority—" Johnson broke in.

"Oh, I understand that," Jessie interrupted. "But I'll have to think about your proposal. And more important, I'll have to see your diamond field with my own eyes before I make any sort of decision."

"Well, that's what we're here for," Powell broke in. "Just like we told you when we talked before, we don't have a thing to hide. And we're ready to take you and show you what we've uncovered. You say the word when."

"Ki and I are ready to leave tomorrow, if that suits you," Jessie said. "I understand it's not too far from here?"

"Not far at all," Benson replied. "It's only a two-day ride, if we keep moving fairly well."

"Then suppose we do just what you gentlemen have already half-planned," Jessie said. "Since I've seen so many more of your diamonds, including that unusually large one, what I'll need to do now is to get some idea of how difficult it will be to work the claim."

None of the three men spoke for a moment as they exchanged glances, then Johnson took up the conversation. "You won't mind if we ask you to keep quiet about exactly where the valley is?"

"Of course not, Mr. Johnson," Jessie replied. "I'm not accustomed to gossip about my financial affairs."

Johnson nodded to Benson, who picked up the conversation at once. "There's just one more thing we might better tell you before we start out, Miss Starbuck. The deposits we've found in the past few weeks indicate that the diamond field is much bigger and richer than we'd figured it to be, before John and Tek visited you at your ranch. Perhaps twice as big."

"That is good news," Jessie replied. "Will tomorrow be too soon for us to start? I'm getting quite anxious to see this discovery you've made."

"Tomorrow's fine with us," Johnson replied. "The sooner we get there and close a deal for you to come in with us, the quicker we'll all be richer than we are right now."

"What's your opinion, Ki?" Jessie asked as they reached the head of the stairs. The diamond promoters had adjourned to the saloon next door to the hotel after their conference with Jessie was concluded.

"It's just what it was before," Ki replied. "And I'm sure yours is, too."

"It is," Jessie said, nodding. "I've had enough experience with confidence men to know one when I see him. These three are a bit smoother than most, and they've certainly got a lot more imagination. But they're con men, just the same."

"How long are you going to play them along?"

"Until we get a look at this diamond field they keep dangling in front of me. I can come very close to telling you what their plan is, and after the years you've spent with Alex and with me, you should know what their next move will be."

"Oh, I think I do," Ki replied. "They've planted a few big pockets of diamonds on that claim. They'll let you find one or two of them—accidentally, of course. Then they'll come up with a figure of how much money will be needed, and push you to buy up all the stock. Finally, just as soon as they get your money, they'll vanish into thin air, and you'll be left holding a lot of worthless land in the Arizona desert."

"Yes, that's how I'm sure they're planning to handle their little game," Jessie said with a smile. "There's just one thing you've failed to add to your story, Ki. When the swindlers leave the claim they've sold me with my money in their pockets, they'll walk right into the arms of the sheriff."

Ki smiled. "It'll be interesting to see if they follow the pattern." While talking they'd walked along the corridor to the doors of their rooms. "But right now, I'm more interested in bed than in diamonds. Good night until breakfast, Jessie."

“Good night, Ki,” Jessie replied. She entered her room and closed the door.

Ki unlocked the door of his own room and went inside. The room was in darkness, and he took a match from his pocket while he groped for the lamp on the table beside his bed. Before he could strike it a hand closed over his wrist.

“Don’t, Ki,” a woman’s voice said softly. It came from the bed, “We won’t need a light, at least not now. Don’t you realize how long I’ve been waiting here for you?”

Chapter 9

Ki recognized the voice at once. He said, "I wasn't really expecting a visitor, Callie Mae."

"I don't suppose you were, Ki. But when we were on the way back from the old pueblo, you'd've turned sorta red in the face if I'd told you I'd made up my mind to come visit you here in your room. It might not've set so well with that Starbuck lady you work for, and she was listening to everything we said."

"I doubt that Jessie would've been embarrassed, but perhaps it's just as well that you didn't say what you were planning to do," Ki agreed.

"I had a pretty good idea you wouldn't exactly be mad if we ran into each other again," Callie Mae went on. "I sorta thought you might come visit me at the saloon, and I waited a pretty good while, but you didn't come in. So I figured I'd have to be the one to make the visit. You are glad I did, aren't you?"

"Of course I am. But I'm surprised, too."

"To tell you the truth, Ki, I'm a little bit surprised myself. Not that it makes any difference, now I'm here.

But you act like you're afraid to come close to me, I came here because I wanted to, but if you don't want me to stay—"

"Of course I do!" Ki broke in to assure her. "I suppose I'm just a little slow in realizing that you're here."

"I figured the way you kept looking at me out in the old pueblo today was all the invitation I needed," Callie said with a smile. "And I'd've done something more than just say thank you right then and there, if your boss hadn't been with us."

While Callie Mae was talking, Ki had been moving closer to the bed. He sat down on its edge beside her, and she slid closer to him. Ki's vision had adjusted to the room's gloom by now. He could see Callie Mae's eyes glistening in the faint glow of moonlight that spilled into the room through the window, and caught the glints of gold in her long blond hair that fell beside her cheeks and spilled over her breasts and shoulders. The soft glow from the moonlight outside darkened her blue eyes and emphasized the full curves of her lips.

"I couldn't say thank you the way I'd've liked to, out there today, but there isn't anybody here to keep me from doing it good and proper now," she went on. Then she chuckled and added, "Well, not proper the way some folks think, but I guess you know what I'm getting at."

"I think I do," Ki replied.

Callie Mae's hand had begun to stroke Ki's thigh while they talked. He could feel the warmth of her palm through the thin fabric of his loose trouser leg. Her hand slipped slowly up his muscular thigh and stopped at the bulge of his crotch.

Ki slipped his arm around her shoulders and pulled

her closer to him. He felt her body's warmth now through the thin fabric of his loose blouse, and the continued caresses of her hand on his crotch were having the effect he was sure she intended; he was beginning to have an erection.

Callie Mae suddenly pushed her full breasts against Ki's chest and began to rotate her shoulders slowly. Her breathing was less even now, broken by small throaty sighs. Ki bent to find her lips with his, and Callie Mae's tongue parted them as she thrust it to meet his. One of her hands crept to his crotch, but windings of the narrow silk scarf, the Oriental *cache-sexe* which was Ki's only undergarment, defeated her efforts.

Suddenly she pulled her lips away from his and abandoned her finger explorations long enough to say, "We're not schoolkids playing house, Ki. We can do a lot better than this if we just take a minute to get rid of all these clothes that keep coming between us."

"You're right," Ki agreed. He moved a handsbreath away from her, missing the weight and warmth of her full breasts pressing his chest, and Callie Mae stood up.

While he sat on the bed, she turned to face him fully and wriggled out of her skirt, letting it fall to the floor. Then she skinned her blouse off over her head, shook out her mane of golden hair, and stood naked, like an ivory statue highlighted only by the window's moonglow.

Ki got off the bed and stood beside her while he shed his blouse and stepped out of his loose black trousers. Callie Mae frowned when she saw his *cache-sexe*.

"What in the world have you got on, Ki?" she asked. "I never saw any underpants like those before."

"Not underpants. A scarf. It's what my people wear."

"Show me," she said.

Ki pulled out the end of the long silk scarf and handed it to her. He said, "All you have to do is unwind."

Callie Mae began unwinding the crisscrossing layers of the narrow scarf that wound in layers to cover Ki's crotch and buttocks. She began giggling when she'd removed the first few folds of the layered strip, then as she reached the end of the silken cloth and saw the jutting erection she'd liberated spring up, her eyes widened.

"Oh, my!" she gasped. "It's time to stop playing now. Hurry, Ki! Let's get back on the bed!"

She took Ki's hand and stepped back until her knees touched the edge of the bed. She wrapped her arms around his chest and pulled him with her as she fell backward. His weight did not keep her from reaching down to position him. When Ki felt himself being engulfed by her moist warmth, he did not lunge, but went into her slowly, lowering his hips into the V of her upraised thighs.

"Deeper!" Callie Mae urged. "All of you, Ki! I want all of you inside me!"

Ki completed his deliberate penetration with a lusty thrust, and a throaty sigh of delight escaped Callie Mae's lips. She lifted her hips to welcome his final thrust, then locked her legs around his hips to lock him to her. She did not raise her hips, but rotated them slowly, rocking from side to side.

"I like not being in a hurry," she whispered. "I hope you can go on for a long time this way, because I enjoy it better every minute."

Ki held himself in position while Callie Mae kept up

her rythmic rolling motion, and after she finally slowed the rotation of her hips he began stroking slowly. Callie Mae brought up her buttocks to meet his deliberate thrusts, and after a few moments, when the tempo of her breathing began to increase, he stopped his rhythmic thrusts and held himself buried fully until the little quivers that had been running through her body died away.

When she no longer shivered, Ki went back to stroking, but at a slower and more deliberate pace. Again Callie Mae rose to meet his penetrations. Ki kept to the slower tempo of his lunges, even stopping his withdrawal strokes now and then to bend his head and caress the budded tips of Callie Mae's full breasts with his lips. He moved from one of her rosettes to the other, caressing their tips with his lips and occasionally rasping them softly with his stiffened tongue.

As her excitement increased, Callie Mae began to squirm beneath him. Ki started thrusting faster now, but with the same deep lunges. Strangled gasps began pouring from her throat as Callie Mae twisted her hips and lifted herself with increasing enthusiasm to meet Ki's drives.

"Don't leave me now, Ki!" she gasped. "And don't go slow anymore! Hurry! And go deeper, and faster!"

Ki did as she'd requested. He set a quicker tempo, but still drove each thrust to completion while Callie Mae's quaking intensified and throaty gasps began bursting from her lips in an almost endless stream. Soon her cries became a single ululating column of sound coming from deep within her throat. Callie Mae's back arched and her hips gyrated wildly for several moments. At last she released a drawn-out gasping cry of delight and began quaking wildly, threshing and rising. Then a final trembling shook her body, and Ki felt her suddenly grow limp.

He drove in one last thrust and held himself firmly against her while Callie Mae writhed slowly as she sighed happily. Ki held himself buried deeply in her until the purling moans that had been pouring from her throat faded and he felt her body soften and go limp. After a few minutes Callie Mae stirred and her eyes opened to look up into his.

"I can still feel you're as big as ever," she said. "I hope that means you can keep on going some more."

"Whenever you're ready," Ki assured her.

"I'm ready now," she whispered. "I didn't think I would be, but I am. And if you keep me feeling the way I do right now, I'm going to stay ready for the rest of the night."

Ahead of the short string of riders the sun was bathing the low crests of the distant mountains with the last golden rays of daylight. The day had been a long one, and the afternoon had seemed twice as long as the morning.

Shortly before noon the little group had turned away from the low jagged barren hills that rose on the south bank of the Gila River and started across the flat which now surrounded them on all sides. Jessie had turned in her saddle to look back several times when they'd changed directions, but after they'd traveled the dozen or so miles that cut off the horizon for a viewer on horseback the gray-green hillocks that marked the river's course had dropped below the horizon.

Now the horizon-line was almost as straight as a

stretched string and equally as featureless. Almost four hours had passed since Jessie had last seen the dark uneven line that marked the riverbed, a dark wavering half-discernable shadow in the heat-haze that shimmered now in all directions under the light blue sky. With it no longer visible, she lacked a fixed reference point that would give her an idea of how far they'd traveled.

Tek Powell was riding lead, and when they left the river, he'd struck out across the featureless expanse of sun-washed sandy soil that now surrounded them. Jessie was accustomed to flatland, for the Circle Star's range was predominantly level. However, on the big ranch there were mile-long humps and shallow grassed valleys, and no two areas of the spread looked exactly alike. Here there was only the barren sandy soil that stretched without vegetation in gentle featureless undulations that seemed to have no end ahead and no boundaries on either side.

Tightening her reins almost imperceptibly, Jessie let the men in the lead, Powell, then Johnson and Benson, pull slowly ahead of her. She held her mount on the tight rein until she was riding beside Ki.

"If we hadn't done a lot of map-studying before we left the Circle Star, I don't think I'd have the least idea where we are right now," she said. "Let's see if our guesses agree, Ki. As nearly as I can figure, we're somewhere between the Sand Tank Mountains and the Saucedas, even if there's not a rise in sight in any direction we look."

Ki nodded. "That's my idea, too, though I'll admit I don't know how far we are from either range."

"We've covered a good bit of distance, just moving

steadily since we turned south from the river," Jessie went on. "Perhaps as much as twelve or fourteen miles, over this level ground?"

"That's as good an estimate as mine," Ki agreed. "I was thinking twelve, so we're not all that far apart."

"I've discovered one interesting thing, Ki."

"What's that?"

"Powell's going by the compass," Jessie said. "I've seen him look down at his hands at least a half-dozen times."

"In country like this, that's the only thing to go by. I haven't seen anything since leaving the Gila that could be called a landmark."

"You'd think they'd know the country better, or have put out some stakes to mark a trail and make it easier to find their diamond deposits—if they exist at all."

Ki shook his head. "Markers would be an invitation for someone to follow, Jessie. That's the last thing a bunch of swindlers would want to happen."

"I thought of that, but then it occurred to me that they could use a clump of cactus or a big rock or something that would be meaningless to anybody else."

"Meaningless to anybody who didn't know the country," Ki agreed. "But stretches of land like this don't bother anyone who carries a compass and knows the heading to take. It's just like navigating a ship in the ocean, Jessie."

"I hadn't thought of it in those terms. But I haven't done as much ocean traveling as you have, Ki."

"If I were trying to pull off the kind of swindle we're reasonably sure our friends up ahead have in mind, this is the sort of place I'd look for," Ki said thoughtfully.

"When you put it that way, it makes sense," Jessie

agreed. "But I'll have to admit, riding without knowing exactly where you're heading and not having any landmarks to follow isn't my favorite kind of trip."

"We know that we can't be too far from where we're going, Jessie. We know the general direction we've been traveling. If bad comes to worse, we won't have to just flounder around. It'll be easy to find our way back."

Before Jessie could reply, Benson reined his horse around and headed toward them. Jessie and Ki fell silent, waiting. He reached them and reined his horse around to ride beside them.

"I'm sure you've already noticed that this isn't a place for interesting scenery," Benson said, smiling. "But we're almost to the canyon where we made our diamond discovery. It's not much of a place to look at, but there's a little cool-water spring, and we put up a little ramshackle cabin when we found that we'd be there for quite a while. We'll turn the cabin over to you, of course. It'll be a little more comfortable than sleeping on the ground."

"Don't be concerned about our comfort," Jessie told him. "Wherever it is we're going couldn't be any worse than some of the places where Ki and I have made camp."

Benson nodded and went on: "We've managed to build up a pretty good food cache during the time we spent prospecting the canyon, so we won't be hungry. And I don't suppose we'll be there very long, Miss Starbuck. Once you've seen how rich the diamond field is, I'm sure you'll realize that we're offering you a real opportunity."

"Without meaning to offend you, Mr. Benson," Jessie said, smiling, "I've been offered so many 'real opportunities' since my father's death that I've come to be just a little cautious about anything that I haven't seen with my own eyes."

"That's understandable," he said quickly, "And that's why we're glad you've come to look at our discovery. We'll welcome the chance to prove to you that we're not out to involve you in any kind of shady deal."

"How much farther do we have to go?" Ki asked when Benson fell silent.

"Another half-hour ought to see us there," he replied. He pointed to the featureless terrain that stretched in front of them. "Keep your eyes ahead. In another two or three miles you'll see a line of cliffs. That's the eastern boundary of the valley where the diamonds are."

Benson toed his horse around and rode off to join his companions. As he got out of earshot Jessie turned to Ki.

"Our Mr. Benson's very convincing, isn't he?"

"He certainly is," Ki agreed. "He's doing his best to lay the groundwork for the deal you're being offered."

"You know, Ki," Jessie said, frowning, "there are times when I find that I'm almost believing what these men have told us."

"Oh, they're shrewd, Jessie. Swindlers generally are. I went with Alex several times to investigate discoveries that were supposed to've been made by poor starving prospectors, and most of them had done a very artistic job of salting them."

They fell into a companionable silence then as they rode across the sandy terrain in the heat of the declining sun. An hour passed, then another, before Jessie stood up in her stirrups and pointed to the horizon.

"Look, Ki!" she exclaimed. "Those must be the cliffs that Benson mentioned. That means we're almost to the valley."

Following her pointing finger, Ki peered at the eastern horizon, where a dark line was visible through the shimmering heat-haze. As badly blurred as they were by the shimmering air and the distance, he could see the dark line that indicated the bluffs Jessie had noticed.

"I didn't really expect the valley to be as close as it is to a town," he told her. "We're only a bit more than a long two-day ride from Gila Bend."

"This is still one of the most desolate places I've ever been in," Jessie said. "And one of the hardest to get to. But those are certainly cliffs and—" She broke off as one of the men ahead reined around and started toward them. "It looks like we're about to get another sales spiel now," she said to Ki.

This time it was Jack Johnson who rode back. He wheeled his horse and fell in beside Jessie and Ki.

"I suppose you've seen the end of the desert's just ahead," he began. "We'll be at the valley in another hour, at most."

"That's what Ki and I were just talking about," Jessie replied. "And we can't get there too soon to please me."

"I'm afraid you won't find much relief from the heat, Miss Starbuck," Jackson said. "It's even hotter in the valley than it is on this level stretch we're on now. But when you look at it one way, that's all to the good. The heat makes our valley so hard to get to that it's kept prospectors away. If Tek and me hadn't been carrying empty canteens, we never would've stumbled on to the diamond deposits."

Jessie nodded. "I remember what you told us when

we were talking back at the Circle Star. As I recall, you were just about to give up when you saw the cliffs beyond the valley and decided to head there to see if you could find water."

"That's right," Johnson said. "And we did. Just by pure luck. We'd come up from the south, where we'd been prospecting in the Battamote Mountains, and then we'd stopped when we got to the Saucedas."

"But you must've known you were heading for desert country," Ki said, frowning. "Didn't you fill your canteens every time you came across water?"

"Oh, sure," Johnson replied. "But that was real seldom, Ki. I don't suppose you've been across that country to the south of here, or you wouldn't've asked."

"I've never been in that part of Arizona Territory," Ki told him. "But I've seen enough this far north to realize how little water there is."

"We hadn't been here before, either," Johnson said, then continued, "We were pretty bad off for water when we left the Saucedas, but we figured we could tough it out till we got to the Sand Tanks. It turned out we were wrong. Well, we cut across the flatland to make better time, and I don't mind telling you, when we got where we found the first diamond deposit we were a lot more interested in a good drink from the spring it was laying by than we were in what looked like a bunch of rocks a little way past the water."

"That's the way discoveries are made, I suppose," Jessie put in. "It's odd, too, they always seem to be made by some prospector who's out of water or injured or something of that sort, and he makes a discovery just by accident."

"That's the way it was with us," Johnson agreed. "It

sure wasn't anything we were looking for. And I'll tell you, Miss Starbuck, when we get a little bit farther on to the place where we've been exploring, you're going to be the most surprised lady in the country when you get a look at what we found."

"Unfortunately it looks like we won't get a chance to see anything tonight." Ki interrupted. "It's getting too late to do much other than camp out for the night."

"Ki's right." Jessie agreed. "Let's spread our bedrolls as soon as we get to the valley."

Chapter 10

"Well, Miss Starbuck, now that we've all had a good night's sleep, I hope you feel up to doing a little walking," Harvey Benson said as the group sat in the crowded little shanty eating breakfast. "If you do, I'd like to show you some of our discovery claims."

"I certainly feel like getting on with what we came here to do," Jessie replied. "And if it requires walking, that's the best way I know of to get rid of saddle stiffness."

Benson waved toward the open door. Dawn was just beginning to become daybreak. Except for a thin strip along the jagged rim of the eastern horizon, the sky was not yet fully bright. There was even a narrow rectangular line at the very top of the doorway where a tinge of the deeper blue of night was still visible.

"We'll see the sun coming up before too long," he went on. "And once it hits the floor of the sink, it's not more'n a matter of an hour or so before the ground gets hot enough to burn your feet right through your bootsoles."

"Then by all means, let's start now," Jessie told him. "I don't suppose you'll object to Ki going along with us?"

To Jessie's surprise, Ki spoke before Benson could reply. He said, "If you don't mind, Jessie, I'd rather stay here. I think I might have gotten a little bit too much sun, riding all day yesterday and the day before."

"You're not ill, are you, Ki?" Jessie asked.

"Don't worry, I'm not feeling really bad. But I think it'd be better if I don't spend another day in the sun right now."

"Stay here by all means, then," Jessie insisted. "This sink isn't all that big. If you need anything, fire a shot in the air and I'll get back here right away."

"I'll be all right," Ki assured her. "I'm not really sick or anything like that, but the best way to keep from getting sick is to be careful right now."

"We'll look out for Ki, Miss Starbuck," Tek assured Jessie quickly. "Me or John will see to it that one of us stays close by the cabin, in case he needs some help."

She nodded and turned to Benson to say, "I suppose we'd better get started, then. Will we need our horses?"

"Our feet'll be good enough. It's not all that far." While he was talking, Benson strapped on a wide belt with a canteen attached to it. He hunkered down beside a short-handled prospector's spade and pickaxe that lay beside him and slid their handles through leather loops in the back of the belt. "I'm all tooled up," he went on. "Ready to start when you say the word."

Jessie picked up her broad-brimmed hat and settled it on her head, then followed Benson outside into the beginning day. The eastern sky was brighter now, and the strip of night-blue had almost totally disappeared. Only a thin line of azure darker than the washed-out blue of the rest of the heavens remained as a reminder of the night.

"I'll take it just as easy as I can, Miss Starbuck," Benson assured Jessie as they started across the rocky soil. "We sampled a few spots that looked promising before we took off to go look for somebody to help finance us, so we won't have to waste a lot of time looking for places to dig, we'll know just where to head for. We ought to be back here by the middle of the morning, before the day really hottens up. And we'll take it nice and easy."

"I don't imagine that I'll have any trouble keeping up with you," Jessie replied. "I manage to stay in pretty good shape just by the work I do on the Circle Star. But of course, that's all on horseback."

"About the main thing to remember in desert country like this is not to get dried out," Benson went on. "But there's plenty of water in this canteen I'm carrying, and there's some water at two or three places in the valley here where a little wet spot's formed by what we've called sinks, for lack of a better word."

"Oh, I know what sinks are," Jessie said, nodding. "We have a few of them on the Circle Star. The ones there are formed by a trickle of water underground."

"Then you'll know what I'm trying to describe. These are small, of course, but if you dig a couple of handfuls of dirt from one of them and wait a few minutes, a little water seeps into the hole. It's not drinking water, but if you splash it on your face, it'll cool you off and keep you from getting sunstroke."

Jessie nodded agreement. She was already feeling the air beginning to warm up. There was no real breeze, but now and then Jessie was sure she could feel a tiny trace of motion, more an air current than a breeze.

"This hat I've got on isn't exactly the best protection from the sun," she went on. "But it's the only hat I have with me. Can you give me some idea of how far we'll be walking? Not that it matters, but I'm a bit curious. I'm anxious to see what you and your friends have discovered."

"What I've got in mind is to show you three or four of the places where we've found sinks," Benson answered. "There's one not too far ahead. In fact, it's the place where Jack and Tek found the first diamonds. I'm pretty sure they didn't work it so hard that they took all the diamonds out. My guess is there's quite a few left in it."

They walked on in silence for perhaps a quarter of an hour, following no track or trail that Jessie could see, then Benson touched her arm and pointed ahead. Jessie saw nothing unusual when she glanced in the direction he'd indicated. The whitish-hued ground looked the same everywhere. She saw a few small boulders and a scattering of fist-sized to thumb-sized rocks, but nothing that seemed to be significant.

"Perhaps I don't understand yet what I'm supposed to be looking for," Jessie said, frowning. "Didn't you mark your claims with location stakes?"

"There wasn't any need to. I was here to chase away any claim-jumpers. Now look closer at where I'm pointing."

Jessie scanned the ground in front of them and shook her head. She said, "I certainly don't see anything different from the rest of the valley."

"Neither did I, when I first joined Jack and Tek,"

Benson told her. "But if you'll look at that biggest outcrop, you'll see there's some loose dirt scattered around close to it. That's the first sinkhole they ran into."

They'd continued walking while they talked and were now only a few paces from the half-buried boulders. For the first time Jessie could see some scatterings of small pebbles and a few areas where the topsoil looked rough and grainy in contrast to the surrounding area.

A few more steps took them to the spot and now Jessie could see a small excavation that had been hidden by the rising hump of the calf-high boulder.

"Is this a sinkhole?" she asked.

"It certainly is," he replied. "Jack and Tek had just stopped here to camp overnight—but I think they told you how they made the first discovery."

"Yes. And I can see how it would happen; you saw the ground here looked wet, just as it does now, and your friends just started digging, hoping they'd open up a spring."

"That's right. They were real put out when they didn't strike water and almost left to look somewhere else. Then it got to them that what they'd taken for pebbles and just shoveled aside had a sort of glowing look. That got their attention, and they tried to break a few. It wasn't until they showed me their samples and I found out how hard the stones were that all of us realized what they'd found were diamonds."

"I don't suppose you've had time to prospect the rest of the valley yourself?" Jessie asked.

"Not the way it needs to be prospected, Miss Starbuck. But after I got here, I knew better than to take what they'd found for some sort of fluke. We started looking for other places like it, and sure enough, there were a lot of 'em. But we still haven't gone over the whole valley like we ought to."

"And from the looks of the ground around this one, I'd say you didn't really dig very extensively here."

"Not by a long shot. We just sorta poked around, here and at two or three of the other places we've found just like it."

"I'm going to need some kind of proof—or verification, if you want to be fancy, that there are other deposits in the valley," Jessie said thoughtfully.

"Why, that's no trouble. Jack and Tek ran across six or seven other holes just like this one before I got here. They were really stirred up about what they'd uncovered after I told them they'd run into a diamond deposit."

"Then suppose we look at a few of the other holes you've tested," she suggested.

"That's what we set out to do," Benson said. "But don't you want to take a closer look at this one, before we move on? I'm pretty sure they didn't take time to clean out all the diamonds that're in it."

"As long as we're here, I suppose I'd better," Jessie agreed. "Will you do the digging, or shall I?"

"Now, that's up to you, ma'am. I'll be glad to, but if you want to be sure that we're not just spinning a tall yarn, it might be better if you dig yourself. It's not hard. The dirt around this place is dry and loose."

"Then if you'll let me have your tools, I'll try my hand," she said. "But I'm not used to handling a spade with such a short handle."

"It'll come easy, when you get the hang of it," he assured her, freeing the spade from its carrying loop and handing it to her. "All you'll need to do is just scratch around. We loosened the dirt pretty good, it oughtn't be bad."

Jessie was not accustomed to digging, especially with a short-handled spade that was designed to be used when kneeling. She worked clumsily and slowly at first, one hand often getting in the way of its mate, until she found the balance points on the tool's handle. Once she'd learned to keep her hands in the same place while driving the blade into the ground she found the self-imposed job easier.

Jessie had created a hole as large around as a big dishpan and as deep as the length of the spade's blade when she struck firmer soil. In the heavier, less sandy soil the digging became more difficult than before. The earth she encountered now was packed more solidly, and soon it became necessary for her to drive the blade into the soil twice before she could force its sharp edge deeply enough to remove more than a few handfuls of the strange whitish dirt.

Benson was quick to notice the increasing difficulty Jessie was having. A frown flicked across his face, and he hunkered down beside her at the rim of the little excavation she'd succeeded in creating.

"That's a funny thing," he said. "There ought to be a few stones left in here. I'm sure Jack and Tek couldn't've taken out the entire deposit. They didn't get down as deep as you've dug."

"Perhaps they took out more stones than they remember."

"It's possible, of course. After they realized what they'd stumbled over, I'm sure they weren't paying too much attention to anything but seeing how many more they could find."

"That's understandable," Jessie said. "I'm sure that all of you were pretty excited about what you'd uncovered."

"Well, there's not any use in tiring yourself out so early in the day, Miss Jessie," Benson went on. "Maybe you'd better give me the pick. I'll do the digging, and you just break up the dirt clods and look for diamonds."

Jessie was glad enough to step out of the small shallow excavation and hand the spade over to her companion. He kneeled at the edge of the hole she'd started and began making the dirt fly. From time to time Benson stopped to break up a clod that he'd lifted out, but not a pebble showed up.

"I just don't understand this," Benson said, frowning as he stood up and gazed down at the small excavation. "But as you know yourself, Miss Jessie, mining's a chancy proposition. I might hit a pocket the next shovelfull I turn, or I might have to go down another foot or so before hitting a deposit. I think the best thing for us to do is move to another spot. I won't even cover up this dry hole we've hit. We can do that later."

"Whatever you think best," Jessie agreed. "Perhaps a move will change our luck at that."

They struck out, Benson taking the lead by a half-step. He moved across at right angles to the hole they'd been exploring. The sun had risen above the rim of the valley by this time, and the light breeze that had rippled across the valley had now died completely. As chancy as its small riffles had been, Jessie missed its cooling touch. She tilted her hat to shade her face and kept pace with Benson until he stopped beside another small patch of disturbed earth.

"Suppose we try here," he suggested. "It's one of the

real shallow test-holes that Jack and Tek put down. Of course, I looked at it, just like I did the others, but I didn't do any digging. They'd put down enough test-holes to satisfy me that they'd uncovered an extensive diamond deposit."

"But they did get some diamonds out of here?" Jessie asked.

"I'm sure you can't have forgotten what Jack and Tek told you when they visited you," Benson replied. "They found at least a few diamonds in almost every test-hole they dug."

"No, I haven't forgotten," Jessie assured him. "And I can understand why you felt so frustrated when the hole we dug back there didn't have any in it."

"Would you like to do a bit more digging, or shall I?"

"If it's all the same to you, Mr. Benson, I'll let you handle the shovel," Jessie answered. "I'll have to admit that digging isn't one of my favorite occupations. Give me a good horse and a lariat, and I'm at home. Diamond mining is strange to me."

Benson frowned. "But I understood that you inherited a number of mining properties from your father."

"Gold, silver, and copper," Jessie explained. "But diamonds—well, I've never even been near a diamond mine."

"This will be a real opportunity for you, then, Miss Starbuck. Since you've been managing the mining properties you inherited from your father, you'd certainly know more about the job than any of us."

"I can't say that yet," Jessie said, frowning. "Until I've satisfied myself that there are diamonds here, I'm not making any plans."

"I'm sure that when you see gemstones such as the

few samples you've looked at, you'll welcome the opportunity this diamond field offers," Benson said. "But here we are talking when I should be digging."

Taking his shovel from its carrying loop, Benson began to dig in the broken patch of soil. He moved carefully, raking with his fingers through each spade-load of earth he lifted. Two or three times he found a small pebble, which he wiped and examined closely before discarding it.

Jessie was watching him closely, noticing the frown of bewilderment that had spread over his face when he'd removed all the loosened dirt from the hole and had started to remove clods of solid dirt that had not been broken previously. He'd controlled his expression quickly, but Jessie had not missed the beginning of his frown.

"I'm dogged if I can figure this out," Benson told her after emptying his spade on the small heap of earth which had resulted from his efforts. "But there's one more place close by where we made a find. Let's give it a try. If it turns out to be like these we've tried, I think we'd better go back to camp and get Jack or Tek to come back with us and guide us to a place we can be sure of."

"Were you here all the time while your partners were gone?"

"Sure. Except when I rode in to Gila Bend to find out at the telegraph office if they'd sent me a wire. I had to go twice before I got the message they sent, that they were coming back."

Jessie nodded. "Yes, they were delayed in getting away from the Circle Star. The day they got there we were shipping our market herd, and I couldn't spare any time to visit with them, so they did lose a couple of days."

"I can see what you're getting at, though," Benson went on. "But I wasn't gone all that long, and you'd think I'd notice if there'd been anybody here while I was away."

"Well, suppose we try this one you said is so close," Jessie suggested. "You know the old saying about the third time being a charm."

"I sure hope it works out that way," Benson said, frowning. "The hole I'm thinking about is right over there."

He pointed, but Jessie could not see anything in the area he'd indicated that showed evidence of digging. Nevertheless, she walked along beside him until they reached a patch of earth that was very much lighter than the ground surrounding it. The spot was much smaller than the earth surrounding it, and she had to look much more carefully to distinguish where it ended.

"Do you feel like you'd like to do a little more digging by now, Miss Starbuck?" Benson asked.

"I think I should do it," Jessie replied promptly. "You did most of the work at the other two places we tried."

Benson handed her the spade, saying as he did so, "I'd say to try close to the center of that light-colored patch. From what I found in the other holes John and Tek put down, is that the diamonds were thickest around the middle of these patches of light-colored dirt."

Jessie scanned the soil before she began digging, but if the area had been disturbed, she could see no evidence of it. She chose a spot near the center of the light-colored area and dug in. She did not try to cover as large an expanse as she'd excavated before, and within a few minutes several sizable heaps of fresh dirt rose around her feet.

By this time the heat of the sun had increased enough to make hard work uncomfortable. Even on the warmest summer days on the Circle Star there was generally a breeze, though it was often light and fitful, and the grassy Texas rangeland did not radiate the sun's heat as did the barren soil of the big sink.

While Jessie dug, Benson had been kicking at the clods she tossed from the shovel, breaking them up with his feet. Jessie had excavated a hole the diameter of a big dishpan and half again as deep when he called to her, "Stop digging and come take a look here, Miss Starbuck. I think you've unearthed a diamond or two."

Sticking the spade's pointed blade into the bottom of the hole she'd excavated, Jessie stepped up beside Benson. He was wiping a small pebble with his fingers to remove the few bits of dirt that still clung to it. He finished wiping and handed her the stone.

"Hold it up to the sun," he suggested. "Even when they're not completely cleaned, there'll be some light passing through that stone, if I'm right about it being a diamond."

Jessie had been turning the misshapen pebble in her hands, trying to remove the last vestiges of earth. She did as Benson had suggested and held it up to the sun. She thought, but could not be sure, that the bit of pale grayish rock was slightly translucent. The sun's glare was bringing tears to Jessie's eyes by the time she'd stared at the pebble for a few seconds. She dropped her upraised hand and shook her head.

"I can't be sure about this stone," she told Benson. "Just when I'm getting my eyes fixed on it, they start watering."

"We can spare enough water to wash it," Benson suggested. He took the cap off the canteen and dribbled a few drops into his cupped palm, rubbed the water on the stone, and dried it on his shirtsleeve. He held it between his eyes and the sun, then handed it back to Jessie.

She did as Benson had, held up the small irregularly shaped pebble and glanced at it with her eyes closed to slits. It did seem to be opaque when she looked at it, but a clouded opacity rather than a clear one. Her eyes began watering again, and blinking did nothing to rid them of the tears gathering in them.

"I—I think you're right," she said. "But I still can't be sure of anything."

"Try again," Benson suggested. "But hold the stone to catch the sun without your eyes in its full glare."

Jessie did as he'd suggested, and this time, with the sun at an angle instead of shining full in her face, she was reasonably certain that she could see the stone was translucent. Turning back to Benson, she said, "I'm pretty sure by now."

"And I'm very sure," Benson replied. "Congratulations, Miss Starbuck. You've just found your first diamond!"

Chapter 11

"You're positive about that?" Jessie asked incredulously.

"Very sure indeed," Benson said with a nod. "It's smaller than most of those that we uncovered when we were trying to learn the lay of the land so we could stake our discovery claims, but it's a diamond, all right."

"Even if you weren't so sure, finding even this one stone beats digging up a lot of dirt with no stones in it at all," Jessie told him. "It encourages me to look for more. Is there another place close where you and your friends found diamonds?"

Benson glanced around at the featureless terrain, then lifted his eyes to the rim of the valley and turned his head as he started to scan it. Suddenly he dropped his head and returned his attention to Jessie.

"I seem to remember another one that's not too far away," he said. "But after looking at so many parts of this sink, I just can't recall exactly where. Tek and Jack would be the ones to know better than I do. They did most of the digging and exploring while I was busy checking over the stones they'd already found."

"Didn't you mark claims for the places where you found a diamond deposit?"

"We knew better than to do that, Miss Starbuck. Nowadays, when you're prospecting and you make a strike, it's not always good business to stake out a claim."

"I've always thought that staking one was the way to keep other miners from claiming an ore deposit you've discovered."

"Maybe that was the case during the first gold rush out here in the West. From what I've heard and read, the old forty-niners were mostly honest, but it's not the same today."

"You mean that there are a lot of claim-jumpers around?"

"More than I like to think about," Benson nodded. "The seventy-three panic's been over a long time, but what happened during it was pretty much the same thing that I've heard was common during the forty-niner days. A lot of crooks moved west because they figured they could get by easier out here than in big cities with police forces, then when they found that the West had police forces too, they headed for the gold fields."

"And a lot of them stopped in cattle country, too," Jessie added. "But perhaps it would be a good idea to put off looking for anything else right now. There'll be plenty of time later on, and I'm sure the diamonds won't grow legs and walk off."

Though their search had not taken Jessie and Benson a great distance from the shanty, by the time they reached it the sun had climbed higher in the cloudless sky and the air had gotten uncomfortably warm. The early-morning breeze had died, the earth was once again beginning to radiate heat, and Jessie was glad to get into the only shade offered—inside the cabin.

"Miss Starbuck has found her first diamond," Benson announced the instant they'd stepped inside. "It took her a while to run across one, though."

"There's a lot more where that one came from, too," Tek told Jessie. "But I can't figure why you didn't uncover more. There's sure plenty of them out there."

"If they're there, they're a lot harder to find than I thought they'd be," Jessie said. "Why, the first place we looked, there wasn't anything but dirt, not even any common pebbles."

Ki was hunkered down beside the wall of the cabin, fining-up the edge of his *ko-dachai* with the small whetstone he carried in his saddlebags. So far he'd said nothing beyond joining the others in greeting Jessie and Benson when they first entered. Now he laid the whetstone aside and stood up, the fighting-knife still in his hand.

"Have you tested the diamond, Jessie?" he asked.

"Of course. Mr. Benson showed me how to hold it up to the sun. Even if it hasn't been cut yet and the outside's rough, you can see that the inside is just clear as the air. I'm sure he's right about it being a diamond, Ki."

"Let me give it another test, then," Ki suggested. He held out the *ko-dachai* and went on: "You know how hard the steel of my *ko-dachai* is, Jessie. If the stone you found will scratch its blade, then you can be even more certain than you are now that you've found a diamond."

Without hesitation Jessie handed Ki the small stone

she'd discovered. Gripping it firmly in his iron-hard fingertips, Ki pressed the stone against the side of his knife-blade and dragged it along the side of the shining steel. There was a small squeak as he drew the stone down the knife, and behind it they could see a small shallow scratch.

"What do you say now, Ki?" Jessie asked. "Mr. Benson was right. It is a diamond!"

"So it is," Ki agreed. "Perhaps you'd have found some more if you'd looked longer."

"We'd already looked a long time, and this was the only diamond we found." Jessie frowned. "And Mr. Benson dug at two other places while I sifted the soil. There wasn't even a common everyday pebble in either one of them."

"You sure about that, Miss Starbuck?" Johnson asked almost before Jessie had stopped speaking. A frown on his face, he turned to Benson and asked, "Did you take her to the holes where we got all those diamonds that me and Tek carried back East to show what we'd found?"

"We went to both of them," Benson replied quickly. "And what I think has happened, Jack, is that when we were gathering those samples, we cleared out the pockets pretty well."

"Sure," Tek chimed in. "That's the only way you could account for not finding anything in either one of 'em. I'll bet if we went back and dug deeper we'd come up with a lot of diamonds that we just didn't go down far enough to find."

"Tek's right," Johnson joined in. "When we were looking for samples, we just sorta skimmed the top. As I recall, we didn't dig deep at all."

"We can always go back to those old holes and dig

deeper," Tek repeated. There was a bit more emphasis in his voice than was needed to make his point. "We know there's more where the samples we took came from."

"Sure," Johnson agreed. Then he looked from Tek to Johnson and went on: "We'll wait until the sun starts down to do that, though. Now, how about you two giving me a hand with watering the horses? There's been plenty of time for the well to fill up since we drew the water for our breakfast coffee."

"A well?" Jessie asked. "I haven't seen any sign of one close by. I thought all the water we had was in our canteens. Where is your well?"

"Just about the last place you'd think to look for it," Tek said with a smile. He stepped to the corner of the cabin and bent down, then pulled up a trapdoor that Jessie had not noticed before. Then he went on, "That's why we built this cabin here where it is, Miss Starbuck. We set it real careful, so it'd cover up the well and hide it from any jackleg desert rat of a prospector that might run across it."

"Not that it's such a much of a well, Miss Starbuck," Johnson put in. "But it's all the water there is hereabouts. And it keeps the space underneath the floor cool enough so we can put away our grub down here, too." As he spoke Johnson was pulling out a bulging flour sack. "Even if summer sausage and cheese is about all we got."

"It serves us," Tek said. "Even if you do have to wait nigh on to half a day after you draw a bucket of water before you can get another bucketful. And once you're used to it, the water don't taste bad at all."

Jessie stepped over to the trapdoor and glanced down

through the opening. She saw that a small hole had been dug in the earth below and also saw the glint of water winking from a circle not much bigger than the tin bucket which stood in the corner.

"It didn't occur to me that there was any water here except what we brought in our canteens," she remarked.

"It's more a hole than a well, and you sure can't draw a tubful of washing-water outa it," Tek said. "But there's plenty to keep our whistles wet, and to make a pot of coffee every morning."

"And just enough to let the horses soak their guzzles once a day," Johnson added. "That's why we don't use 'em any more than we have to, you see." He turned to Tek and Benson and went on: "I'll get the nosebags and we'll take care of the nags."

"It takes all three of us to handle the job," Tek explained to Jessie. "And when we got five nags to water instead of three, and not enough nosebags to let 'em all drink at the same time, the ones that don't get to drink first act so ornery that they got to be held back."

"I'll certainly have to give all three of you credit for being very ingenious," Jessie said with a smile.

"Well, thanks," Benson said. "We'll sorta share your compliment, Miss Jessie."

When the trio had left carrying their watering gear, Jessie turned to Ki and said, "Do you think it takes all three of them to handle the horse watering, Ki?"

"No," he replied promptly, peering out of the open doorway. "But I think perhaps I can get close enough to hear at least part of what they're saying."

"How? The ground outside this cabin is as bare as a baby's bottom, any way you look."

"But I don't intend to go outside," Ki responded.

"And unless they whisper, I think they'll be close enough for me to hear most of what they say while they're watering the horses."

Jessie frowned. "I still don't see how."

Ki stepped up to the trapdoor and peered down. He went on: "There's not much space between the floor and the ground, but I think I can worm and scrape to the other corner. I don't think it's too far from the hitch-rack for me to hear what they say."

While he'd been speaking, Ki had started to lever himself down into the trapdoor opening. With the skill of the master *ninja* that he was, he slipped into the narrow space between the ground and the cabin's floor. It was a very tight squeeze, but by pressing himself close to the loose, shifting sandy soil below the floor and clearing away the high spots in the loose sand as he moved, he found that he could twist and worm his way across the slitlike space.

Being careful to move noiselessly, he wriggled snake-like to the wall nearest the hitch-rack. His hands often encountered nets of cobwebs between the floor joists as he pulled himself along, and occasionally a small shower of dust sprinkled him, but he paid no attention to the small distractions.

When he reached his objective, Ki began scooping away the sand until he'd created a small gap between the bottom edge of the cabin's board siding and the hitch-rack that was now only three or four paces from his hiding place behind the cabin wall.

Pressing his head down into the excavation he'd created, Ki recognized Benson's voice saying, ". . . and when the Starbuck dame didn't find hair nor hide of those diamonds we salted the place with, I felt like I was up shit creek without an oar or a push-pole. Damn it, what kind of fool mistake did you two make?"

"We must've put fifteen or twenty of those diamonds in that one place, Harve!" Tek Powell replied.

"That's right," Johnson seconded. "Just what you told us to do. 'Put plenty in that first place,' you said. And that's what we did!"

"Then how come she didn't find any of 'em?" Benson demanded angrily. "You said there wasn't any at the next place we salted, and I'll swear we planted a handful there!"

"Don't ask me why she didn't find but one," Johnson retorted. "We did just what Tek said we did. We even left a lot of shovel marks at that first place, like you told us to, so the Starbuck woman would be sure to see 'em."

"Well, all I know is that there wasn't one single damn diamond there!" Benson snapped. "She dug all around everywhere, and I helped her go through every shovelful of dirt she lifted, and if there'd been any stones there, I'd've seen 'em!"

"Now, let's not get into a wrangle out here!" Tek begged his companions. "If we start yelling, the Starbuck dame and that slant-eyed servant of hers will hear us!"

"Tek's right," Johnson seconded. "As I see it, there's only one thing that could've happened. Somebody came along here and stole the diamonds."

"Somebody?" Benson snapped. "Somebody who?"

"How the hell do I know who?" Johnson shot back.

"Well, it sure wasn't Santa Claus or the Easter Bunny!" Benson was almost snarling with anger. "It had to be somebody that was watching us when we planted 'em, and if there'd been anybody snooping around while we were salting those holes, we damn sure would've seen 'em!"

"Wait a minute!" Tek said. "Something just popped into my head."

"Well, pop it out!" Benson commanded. "And quick! We can't stay out here arguing much longer!"

"That fellow that was in the stagecoach with me and you on the way to the railhead, John," Tek went on, "the one that got on the stage with us in Gila Bend, and then after we got on the train to Texas and looked for him, we never did see him?"

Johnson did not reply for a moment, then in a somewhat uncertain voice said, "Sure. I guess I do. You mean the one that slept a lot and talked damn little when he was awake?"

"That's him!" Tek agreed.

"What about him?" Benson asked.

His voice thoughtful, Tek went on: "Just figure for a minute what he might've heard me and John saying, if he was just playing possum."

"You mean you two talked about what we had schemed up where somebody could hear you?" Benson demanded.

"Damn it, Harve, the son of a bitch was asleep!"

"Or you thought he was!" Benson snapped. "I guess you went over our whole scheme while this fellow was sitting by you?"

Tek did not reply at once, but after a moment of silence Johnson said, "I guess we did at that."

Listening in his hiding place under the cabin, Ki could visualize Benson's expression from the tone of his voice.

"You talked about salting the place with diamonds?" he asked, incredulity coloring his words.

"Some," Tek admitted. "I don't recall every word we said, but I remember we did say something about how much we had to pay in Juarez for the uncut diamonds."

"And you talked about salting the flats?" Benson pressed.

"Sure. Our backs were still stiff after all the digging we'd had to do," Johnson replied defensively.

"And I remember you've already said this fellow had got on the stage at Gila Bend," Benson went on. "I suppose you talked a lot about where we were staying?"

"As I recall it now, we said something about it," Johnson agreed.

"Well, you damned constipated jackasses!" Benson exploded. "And you wonder why the Starbuck dame didn't find any of the diamonds we planted! Hell, that son of a bitch that heard you two yattering on that train just turned around and came back here and dug up our diamonds! Then he smoothed over the ground like we'd done when we hid 'em, so we wouldn't know he'd been here!"

"Now, wait a minute!" Tek protested. "How was we to—"

"Shut up!" Benson snapped. "We've got to cut this short and get back in the cabin before the Starbuck dame starts wondering what's taking us so long to water the nags."

"Say whatever else is on your mind, then," Johnson suggested. "Because we haven't got any more diamonds to use for bait, and we're sure not—"

"Keep quiet and listen!" Benson commanded. "You're wrong about us not having any more diamonds,

Jack. We've still got the bag of bait we took back to Texas. Now, one of us has got to go out tonight and salt three or four places, ones she hasn't looked at yet."

"You think she'll still fall for it?" Tek asked.

"She damn well better!" Benson snapped. "And this time I'll be along when we take her out to look at what we've planted, you can be sure of that."

"It just might work," Johnson said. "It's worth a try."

"It'd better be worth more than that!" Benson told his companions. There was no mistaking the threat in his voice.

"I don't see how we can miss," Tek broke in. "It'll be a little bit clumsy working in the dark, but we can get the job done easy enough."

"If you think it's all that easy, you take care of it, then," Benson agreed. "There better not be two of us missing, though. If anything should happen that'd rouse us, she'd be sure to notice and start asking questions."

"We going to sleep outside, like you said, and leave the cabin for the Starbuck woman?" Tex asked.

"Sure," Benson said. "I didn't plan it for what we've got to do, but sleeping outside's going to make it easier for one of us to sneak off."

"All right," Tek told him. "Pass me the stones we used for bait. I'll bide my time and when everything's quiet, I'll go do the job. Only don't look for it to be as the one we did in daylight, when we could see to work."

"I'd do the damn job myself," Benson said. "But if something should happen tonight that'd rouse us—"

Tek broke in: "We see that as easy as you do. I know all the places where we put the bait. I won't have no trouble."

"Steer clear of the two or three places the Starbuck

woman saw today," Benson cautioned. "Use the ones she doesn't know about yet."

"I'm smart enough to figure that out for myself," Tek said. "Give me the rocks. I'll start out soon as everything's quiet."

"I sure do wish we could be certain this new scheme's going to work out," Johnson said. "If something should go wrong twice in a row, it'll be Katy, bar the door!"

"Stop borrowing trouble!" Benson snapped.

"And I'll say amen to that," Tek put in.

"It damn well better work," Benson told him. "Here, you take this bag of stones we used for bait. Now, let's finish watering these nags and get back to the cabin."

Ki had started inching his way back to the trapdoor even before Benson finished speaking. He wormed along as fast as he could, pushing with his feet and pulling himself along by gripping the floor joists. Jessie was still standing beside the trapdoor when he emerged, his black jacket and pants streaked with dust and dirt.

"Did you—" Jessie began. Ki cut her question short.

"I heard all I needed," he said. "Now I've got to get outside before those three come in. If they see me, the dirt and cobwebs I got rubbed into my clothes while I was under the floor will be a dead giveaway."

Without waiting for Jessie to comment, Ki hurried to the door. He got outside into the concealing darkness just as Benson and Johnson and Powell were nearing the doorway on their return from the picket line, and vanished before they could hail him.

A short distance from the cabin Ki stopped and began brushing away the traces of his visit under the cabin floor. Though no breeze rippled the air of the moonless night, the day's heat was beginning to seep slowly away. Ki glanced up at the stars that dotted the heavens as he turned and began walking slowly toward the elongated panel of yellow lantern light that spilled across the ground from the open door of the cabin.

He'd taken only a few steps, his eyes still scanning the heavens, when he saw a reddish glint burst into the sky. For a moment he thought he was watching a meteor or some kind of starfall, but the little dot of red not only grew larger but stayed motionless. He stopped and stood looking at the distant gleam for moment, but it neither moved nor diminished nor grew, and Ki realized that he was looking at a distant campfire. Frowning thoughtfully, he hurried back to the cabin.

Chapter 12

"Are there any ranches to the northeast of the valley?" Ki asked as those inside turned when he came through the door.

Johnson and Powell and Benson all stared at him. So did Jessie. At last Benson spoke.

"There's not a ranch or house of any kind to the east, Ki," he said. "Not for sixty or seventy miles, at least. What gave you the idea there is?"

"There's a light showing in that direction," Ki replied. "It wasn't there last night, so it must be just an overnight campfire. I guess there must be a trail in that direction and somebody's made camp along it."

"Let's step out and take a look," Tek Powell suggested. "I don't recall ever seeing a light east of here."

Ki moved out of the doorway, and the three men and Jessie came out to stand beside Ki. He pointed to the light, though it was plainly visible through the clear air of the desert night.

"I'd guess it's an overnight camp," Powell told them. "But it's not anything for us to worry about. Likely an immigrant wagon stopped when it got dark."

"Is there a road or trail in that direction?" Jessie asked.

"Not one that gets any use," Tek told her. "There's not enough water to wet your big toe in for close to a hundred miles."

"It seems to me there's a cattle trail along here somewhere that was used to drive steer over to Texas," she persisted.

"There was," Johnson agreed. "But it hasn't been used since they finished the railroad line to Texas."

"Besides, in that direction all the country between here and Tucson is mostly Papago territory," Benson put in. "Right now they're mostly peaceful, but the Apaches just south of 'em sure ain't."

"It's too far away for us to worry about, anyhow," Johnson commented. "But it's a campfire, for sure. It glows too red to be anything else."

"Might be a lone prospector wandering around and hoping luck will come down like a lightning bolt tomorrow and make him rich," Tek said. "Anyways, it's too far away for us to worry about." He turned back to the cabin. "And I had too long a day. I'm ready to crawl into my blankets."

"Count me in, too, then," Benson chimed in. "Tomorrow's going to be here before we know it."

"We'll be joining you in just a minute," Jessie said. "I'm not a bit sleepy right now, and I'm sure Ki won't mind staying to keep me company."

"Of course not," Ki agreed. "Besides, it's a lot cooler out here than it is in the cabin, with this night breeze that's beginning to blow."

"Come along, then," Jessie said. "We'll have a little stroll before we go to bed."

• • •

"I didn't like to be so obvious about wanting us to have a private talk," Jessie said in a half-whisper as she and Ki moved away. "But there wasn't any other way I could see to get a minute to talk without them hearing us."

"You did it so nicely that Benson and his friends didn't suspect a thing," Ki assured her.

"I couldn't've gone to sleep without knowing what you overheard while you were listening a while ago," Jessie went on.

As briefly but completely as possible, Ki sketched the conversation that had taken place while Benson and Johnson and Powell were watering the horses.

"So you were right from the very beginning, Jessie," he concluded. "It was just what you'd suspected. This whole thing has been a big swindle those three crooks put together to rob you. They planted a lot of uncut diamonds for you to find."

"Then they're not only crooks, Ki. They're fools. Don't they know that for the past—well, at least much longer than I can remember—crooks have been trying to sell salted claims?"

"Confidence men have their own blind spots, Jessie. You're right, of course. Alex used to get three or four propositions a year, just like you do now."

"Begging letters," Jessie nodded. "And letters offering to make me richer than anybody else."

"And that's the kind of letters I was thinking of. Alex's were always from some con man posing as a poor prospector who'd stumbled onto a rich lode and needed a partner to finance him in working it. He investigated all of them, because such things do happen in real life. But he never did get taken in."

"But if Benson and his partners had finished salting the claim before they came to the Circle Star, what happened to the diamonds they planted for me to find?" Jessie frowned.

"It's pretty obvious that somebody stole them," Ki said.

"But who, Ki?" Jessie frowned, then went on quickly: "Do you think it could be one of the swindlers themselves, stealing from his partners?"

"That's possible, of course," Ki agreed. "But right now I'm inclined to think it might be whoever's camped by that mysterious fire I saw on the rim of the valley."

Jessie shook her head. "If whoever built the fire had anything to do with stealing the diamonds Benson and the others buried for bait, they wouldn't give themselves away."

"I'll admit it'd be unlikely," Ki agreed. "I'm sure the thieves who did that are long gone."

"Then why does seeing the fire seem to bother you so much?"

"Jessie, this place is so far off any road or trail that practically nobody ever passes through it. Of course, whoever's camped by that fire I spotted could be innocent prospectors or immigrants heading for California who couldn't afford to buy a railroad ticket or who've got a wagon loaded with furniture, or it might be a prospector or a desert rat. But it could equally well be some careless crook or a fugitive running from the law."

"But the diamond swindlers didn't seem concerned about it," Jessie said, her voice thoughtful. "Still, I suppose anything's possible."

"Whoever started the fire must have a reason for being there," Ki went on, his voice sober. "All we can be fairly certain about is that while Benson and the others were meeting us in Gila Bend, somebody—maybe whoever it is camped across the sink—came in and grabbed all the diamonds that were planted for you to find."

"They'd have had to be watching while the diamonds were being buried," Jessie said, frowning.

"Oh, I'm sure they were. We may never know how they tumbled to what was going on, but professional thieves have their own way of finding out where there's loot."

Jessie nodded. "We've had that proved to us often enough."

"Yes. Benson's bunch didn't have to be careful when they were setting up their trap for you. My guess is that they let something drop when they were in Gila Bend buying supplies, or—well, there's no point in speculating."

"That fire we saw might have been some totally innocent prospector, of course," Jessie suggested.

"It might," Ki agreed. "But in this isolated place there has to be a reason for somebody to be where we saw that fire."

"You know, Ki," Jessie said thoughtfully, "you've just about convinced me that your idea is right."

"Put yourself in the thieves' place," Ki suggested. "If you'd just gotten away with a trick such as the one that's been played on Benson and his friends, would you run, or would you hang around hoping for another big slice of a rich, free pie?"

"I think I'd be greedy," Jessie replied promptly. "Most crooks are. Yes, it's very probable that the men who stole those salted diamonds are still hanging around!"

Ki nodded. "Hoping they'll be able to get their hands on some more."

Jessie's voice was very businesslike when she went on: "I'm sure we'll learn whether or not we're right when we go to find out about the campfire."

"Not we, this time, Jessie. It's a job for just one of us, and you'll need to be here to keep the swindlers busy. They haven't given up yet, you know."

For a moment Jessie was silent, then she nodded slowly and said, "Yes, I see why it's got to be that way, Ki. When are you going to leave?"

"If there were a moon, I'd leave right away," he replied. "Since there isn't, and I'll be going over strange ground, I won't start until I can see where I'm going."

"This has been a busy day, and it seems that tomorrow's going to be another one," Jessie said. "We'd better get what sleep we can. I suppose you'll be gone before our friends in the cabin wake up?"

"Probably. I'm sure you'll be able to explain why I'm not around."

"Of course. I'll just tell them the truth."

"That's pretty hard to argue against."

Jessie heard reflected in Ki's voice the smile she could not see but knew was on his face. She said, "I won't worry when you just aren't here in the morning. And this is one time when I hope you find some innocent reason for that fire instead of learning that it belongs to a new bunch of crooks about to get mixed up in our affairs."

Ki set out from the cabin when the first hint of dawn was visible above the rim of the sink. He moved with the noiseless skill of the trained *ninja* that he was, carrying his shoes as he picked his way carefully out of the cabin and padded on bare feet across the sand. He moved slowly, pausing at each step to rub a foot over the shallow prints he'd left.

Acting almost by instinct the evening before, he'd noted in his memory the location of the fire he'd seen in relation to the cabin. During the perilous years following Alex Starbuck's murder, when Ki was protecting Jessie from the efforts of the cartel to bring about her death as its merciless members had her father's, caution had become his second nature.

Instead of making a beeline across the barren floor of the sink to the spot where he'd seen the flicker of the fire the evening before, Ki crossed the featureless depression at an angle. His target was a place that would take him to the rim of the sink a mile or so from the exact spot where the red dot had caught his eyes.

There were no barriers to slow him down on the featureless surface of almost colorless sandy soil. To make the best speed possible was Ki's second objective, and he moved across the sink quickly at a gait that was almost a trot.

When he neared the slope that rose at a steep but not precipitous angle from the sink's flat bottom, he angled toward it. During the few minutes that were required for him to mount the rock-studded face of the long incline the sky had grown bright with before-sunrise dawnlight.

When he reached the top of the long slanting rise, he shook the sand from his shoes and slipped them on again before he started around the rim of the sink. Here the ground was firmer, but it was strewn with rocks and cut with gullies that had been formed by wind and the occasional rain that fell on the arid land. Now Ki took extra care not only in following the faint tracks but in watching the firmer but rock-strewn ground on the sink's rim for signs that the mysterious fire of the night before had been rekindled.

In spite of the speed he'd made, Ki was still fresh when he reached the sink's rim. Here the terrain changed from the flat featureless floor of the sink. An occasional flat-topped stone lay on the ground, and a few perched like flattened mushroomtops on jagged pillars of soil that rose above the general level of the whitish earth's surface.

Wind and a rare occasional rainstorm had carved gullies and created high spots in the fragile sandy soil. Most of the eroded creases were shallow and narrow, but now and then some freak in the earth's composition had allowed the forces of nature to create gullies. Ki noted these as he passed, storing into his memory the location of those which were wide enough and deep enough to accommodate a man lying prone and to hide him from sight.

Ki pressed on without stopping. Though he concentrated his attention on choosing the best path to his objective, he flicked his eyes ahead frequently, looking for signs whoever had been camped there the evening before might rekindle the fire that had drawn his attention.

He'd moved steadily for a quarter of an hour when the distant neighing of a horse reached his ears. He came to a halt at once, then resumed his progress. Now, though, he moved more slowly. He edged forward silently, taking full advantage of the creases that cut across the crest.

As he continued his slow advance, Ki began straining to hear any sound that might give him a lead to the location of the unexplained camp on the rim of the sink. With any luck, he told himself, he might also hear something that would give him an idea of the purpose of those who had stopped there.

A whinnying horse not only proved that Ki's hunch had been good, but also gave him the first clue that he'd gotten very close to the place he was seeking. He froze in his tracks and strained his ears for other noises that might make it possible for him to judge the distance that remained between him and his objective. The whinny sounded again, and this time it was followed by a man's voice.

"That damn horse is getting on my nerves!" he said. "Mole, can't you get that nag of yours to keep quiet? You know how far away somebody can hear a horse whinnying. We don't wanta give ourselves away to them down there."

Ki had dropped flat, face down on the ground, though the man who'd spoken was still out of sight. He lay motionless, a dark shadow on the barren soil, while he waited for the outlaws to start talking again.

"If there's any way you can shut up a mare that's calling for a stallion to come breed her, I don't know what it is," the man addressed as Mole replied. "She's going to be that way for a few days, so you might just as well make up your mind to put up with it."

"Maybe you'd like to take care of her yourself, Grizz," a third man put in. "You're always braggin' about what a stud you are." When Grizz only snorted and made no reply, the man went on: "Mole's right. There ain't nothing but a stallion topping her that'll shut off them whinnies. Come to think of it, though, I ain't sure you'd qualify."

"Keep your damn joshing to yourself, Blade!" Grizz snapped. "If that bunch down in the sink finds out we're here, they might start shooting."

"Oh, they're mad enough to shoot, I'd lay odds on that," Mole said. "Ain't no way they couldn't've been, when they found out that them diamonds they'd salted the place with so careful wasn't there any longer."

When Ki heard Mole's words, he suddenly realized that he was listening to the men who'd stolen the salted diamonds, and he also had names to go with the voices. While he'd listened to the trio, he was also fixing their position in his mind. Depending on them to be so engrossed in their conversation that they would fail to notice him, Ki continued his stealthy approach.

He crept silently ahead, bellied down as close as possible to the rough broken ground. He moved only a few inches at a time, careful to lift himself from the rocky soil by bracing on his toes and fingertips to avoid the noise he might make by scraping over a loose rock. Inch by inch, he picked his way closer to the sound of the outlaws' voices.

"Yeah, I'd like to've heard what they was saying," Mole was chuckling. "They done a lot of work getting ready for that dame, whoever she is."

"Whoever she is, she's bound to be rich, too," Blade put in. "Listen here, Mole, we better talk some more about grabbing her the first chance we git."

"Now, I'll go along with Blade on that," Grizz exclaimed before Mole could speak. "If she's rich enough to buy a claim from them three cat-eyes, there's bound to be somebody that'd cough up a good bundle to get her back."

"Well, I ain't stopped thinking about it," Mole replied. "She'd have to be rich as creamed owl-shit for them three fellows to take the trouble of salting that sink the way they did."

"It's just damn lucky for us the way things worked out like they have," Grizz said thoughtfully. "All of 'em pulling out at the same time to go get her and the chink that's with her. It give us all the time we needed to grab the diamonds they'd buried for her to find."

"Luck, hell!" Mole grunted. "What's made all of us rich is them three years behind bars I put in at the pen. That's where I learned about salting a diamond claim."

"Well, I learned a lot from the stretches I put in, but I never learned nothing like that," Grizz observed.

"Maybe you just wasn't lucky in the cellmate you had," Mole suggested. "Now, me, I had one from the diamond country down in the south part of Africa."

"I've heard they dig up a lot of diamonds there," Blade said. "So this fellow learned you about 'em?"

"Seemed like to me that all he talked about was diamonds and how horny he was," Mole chuckled. "I was edgy enough myself, so I steered him to diamonds."

"And you found out how to salt a claim from him?" Grizz asked.

"That and a lot more," Mole answered. "How to tell what kind of dirt to look for 'em in, how to tell a real one from a fake, how they go about cutting and polishing 'em. But the real thing I learned was all there is to know about high-grading and salting and things like that. It ain't such a much of a job if you know how."

Ki decided that he could depend on the outlaws relaxing their vigilance while they were engrossed in their conversation. He edged ahead for several more yards while Mole was talking, and found the scanty cover of a small split in the sunbaked earth. Slipping into the rock-cleft, he flattened himself out as best he could in the narrow confined space. Closer to the outlaws now, he could hear them much more distinctly.

"Well, you're getting a bigger split of the take than me or Grizz," Blade was saying. "Which don't mean I'm mad about it or anything like that, Mole. You got the big share coming to you, fair and square."

"I ain't arguin' against that," Grizz protested. "But I still say we better jump at the chance we got to grab that dame while she's here."

"Me and Grizz is talking the same way," Blade added. "It won't be no trick at all to make her tell us how to go about finding whoever can pay us a damn big ransom to let her go."

"I ain't made up my mind about that being the smart thing for us to do," Mole answered thoughtfully. "If she's rich as we figure, she'll have a lot of friends just as rich, and they'd likely be able to get the government to send a bunch of troops out to find her."

"Well, hell, Mole! We've dodged enough lawmen to know how to steer clear of 'em," Blade said.

"Dodging a sheriff or a constable ain't quite the same as dodging the U.S. Army, damn it!" Mole snapped.

"Soldiers ain't all that hard to get away from," Grizz observed. "I learned that when I was serving a hitch before I deserted. They're just like everybody else—they put their britches on one leg at a time."

"Damn it!" Mole exploded. "I ain't dim-brained enough to start doing something that's liable to set the whole United States Army out after us!"

"But it was you that come up with the scheme to begin with!" Grizz protested.

"Mole's right," Blade broke in quickly. "Kidnapping that woman and holding her for ransom wasn't part of what we planned."

"Planned, hell!" Grizz exploded. "There's not no law I know about that says we can't change our plan if a new idea comes along that's better! What we got to think about right here and now is that we got a chance that's gonna double our take outa this job, maybe more than double it. I say we're damn fools not to take it!"

★

Chapter 13

Ki was certain from the way the argument between the outlaws was going that he'd be safe in moving. It was obvious that the three renegades were too engrossed in their own affairs to be fully alert to their surroundings. Ki resumed his stealthy progress and advanced another few yards. This time the gain was less than he'd secured in his earlier moves, for he was now much closer to the trio and forced to limit his movements to the few swiftly passing seconds when he could be sure they were not likely to spot him.

Even when he'd gotten closer to the three men and found a place where he could stretch out flat behind a low rock outcrop, Ki knew that he must close the gap still further. He was still too far from them to be sure of the accuracy that would be required when the time came to launch his *shuriken*. Measuring the distance with his eyes, he decided after a single quick glance that they would continue to be preoccupied with their discussion long enough to allow him to make one more advance, even if it was only a short one.

Ki had also noticed something else during the few seconds when he was studying his adversaries. As they settled down to begin their confab following the brief argument that had flared up between them, they'd taken positions which put the sun at their backs. Not only had they been careful in positioning themselves, their new vantage points had been chosen to give them a better view of the floor of the sink and the cabin.

They had one disadvantage which would favor Ki's attack. In order to see him plainly or to bring the muzzles of their rifles to bear on him, they would be forced to turn completely around. When they did so, the full glare of the bright morning sun would be in their eyes.

And that's what might make the difference, Ki told himself silently as he studied the strip of rocky ground that still stretched between him and his quarry.

Only a bit more than a dozen yards remained now between Ki and the trio of outlaws, and their attention was concentrated on the sink and the cabin. In his present position, Ki could not see the cabin, but it was obvious to him that the outlaws were studying the terrain that lay between them and their objective.

Mole confirmed Ki's reasoning when he said, "I ain't so sure we can find a way to get across that stretch of bare-ass sand without them fellows in the cabin seeing us."

"Then maybe we better stay up here and wait for 'em to come out," Grizz suggested. "There's three of them and three of us, which comes down to a shot apiece."

"That's easy to say," Blade snapped. "But who's going to get their shots off first? Them or us?"

Mole broke in with an objection. "Damn it, there's too much danger at this long range that we'll kill the woman!"

"We're gonna have to put her away anyhow, sooner or later," Blade reminded him.

"Sure," Mole agreed. "But we don't wanta get rid of her till we've finished with her. My taste don't run to dead meat."

"We ain't got time to waste palavering," Blade told his companions. "Let's make up our minds what to do and then do it!"

"If you wanta know what I think, I'd say wait till they get closer," Mole told his fellows. "Chances are they'll do just about as much moving around as they done before, and sooner or later they'll get in easier range."

Ki chose this moment to narrow the gap that still remained between him and the outlaws. He kept his eyes on the trio as he began a careful noiseless advance. He slanted still closer to the outlaws, taking long silent steps across the sandy stretch that separated him from the upthrust rock outcrop which he'd chosen as his next objective.

He'd covered most of his planned distance and was taking a final long step that would put him within reach of the jagged chunk of stone which rose from the sand. Then he found himself caught up in one of those happenstances that can spoil even the most skillful *ninja* move.

Under his weight the foot Ki had planted so carefully in front of him broke through the crusted sandy soil. Waving his arms with the effort, Ki fought to keep his balance.

Though the noise he made as he struggled was little louder than a whisper, his efforts broke the stillness as effectively as a gunshot would have done. Mole was the first of the outlaws to turn when the grating of Ki's feet broke the almost total silence. The outlaw was drawing as he swiveled around.

Ki was trying to overcome his precarious footing. To keep himself from falling, he'd stretched his arms to the utmost and he was rotating them as well. He tried to bring his hands together to get a *shuriken* from the carrying case strapped to his left forearm, but Mole's revolver was already out of its holster.

Ki saw Mole bringing up his pistol and tried to throw his body to one side, but his enforced awkward posture defeated him. He did not hear the report of Mole's shot, for speeding with the report the pistol-slug struck Ki at the roots of his thick black hair. Its impact cut a shallow groove in his scalp as it plowed through his hair and whistled past him, and his consciousness went with the whistling of the slug.

Ki was toppling forward when Mole fired his second round and its lead went harmlessly wild, but the damage had been done. Ki was already unconscious when he slumped to the ground and lay still.

"I haven't seen hide nor hair of that servant of yours this morning, Miss Starbuck," Benson remarked.

While Jessie had excused herself to step outside "for a breath of fresh air," he and Johnson and Powell had been busying themselves preparing breakfast. They'd lifted the food bag from the space below the cabin's floor and were now taking packages of summer sausages and cheese and soda crackers from the big provisions sack and putting them on the one small table the room held.

"Ki decided to look around the sink while the air's still cool," Jessie replied. "He particularly wanted to look at the place where that fire was burning last night."

"He wouldn't've had to wait but a little bit for us to go with him," Tek put in.

"Don't worry about Ki, he's a grown man," Jessie said. "He doesn't need anyone to wet-nurse him."

"He'll know from last night where to find the grub sack, if he don't get back before we leave, then," Benson said.

"Maybe Miss Starbuck had rather wait for her man to come back, so he can go along with us," Johnson suggested. "And we don't have to be in no rush. The diamonds sure won't grow legs and walk away."

Benson cocked his head inquiringly at Jessie as he asked, "Do you want to wait, Miss Starbuck, so your servant can go with us? A few minutes one way or another won't matter."

"We certainly don't need to wait for Ki on my account," Jessie replied. "The sink's not all that large: I'm sure he'll see us on his way back or we'll see him, and he can join us if he wants to."

"We'll start as soon as we finish eating, then," Benson nodded.

"Breakfast's ready, such as it is," Tek put in. He gestured toward the table as he added, "If you don't care for cheese, help yourself to the sausages."

Benson said quickly, "When we were sure you were going to visit us, we put an order in at the store in Gila Bend for a case of airtights, so we'd have some food fit to offer you, but you got here before they did."

"You don't need to apologize," Jessie said, smiling. "We're as far away from a grocery store at the Circle Star as you are here, and I know how long it takes for our orders to be delivered. But as far as I'm concerned, instead of spending a lot of time eating, I'd rather be looking for more diamonds."

"I hope you won't think I'm stepping over the line when I say what's on my mind, Miss Starbuck." He paused as though waiting for Jessie's permission to go on.

"Please don't hold back your thoughts," Jessie told him.

"When you had such a disappointing day yesterday, I was afraid you might've lost interest," Benson finished.

"It's not that I doubt your word that you've uncovered some valuable diamond deposits, Mr. Benson," Jessie said. "It's simply that I never invest in anything until I'm satisfied the money I put in will return a profit."

"Well, we sure were disappointed yesterday, but we're a long ways from covering the whole sink yet, Miss Starbuck," Benson said. "I've got an idea we might've been in just too big a hurry yesterday to look as carefully as we needed to. Now, I suggest—"

"Wait!" Jessie exclaimed. "I heard gunshots!"

Except for Jessie's keen hearing, the shots fired by Mole might have passed unnoticed inside the cabin, for there they were barely audible. Even to Jessie and Benson, who were standing outside, the two reports were no louder than the snapping of fingers.

"That shooting's on the other side of the sink, where Ki was going!" Jessie exclaimed.

"I'd agree with you," Benson replied. "But we haven't seen a sign of anybody in that direction since we got here. I don't think we need to worry. It certainly can't be anything that concerns us."

"That was the direction Ki was going to look at, and

if those shots concern Ki, they're my concern, too," Jessie told Benson. "You and your men do what you want to. I'm going to find out what's happening!"

"Well, we sure ain't the kind to let you walk off by yourself and maybe bust into a hornet's nest," he assured her. He turned to his companions and went on: "Let's saddle up and go with Miss Jessie. It won't take us long to find out if her man Ki's got hisself into some kinda jackpot, and if he has it won't take long to help her get him outa it."

Consciousness returned to Ki painfully. For the first few moments after he regained his awareness, he made no effort to move, not even to explore the painful area of his head where the pain was centered. He was still lying prone and motionless when the faint scraping of feet approaching reached his ears.

Then he heard the whispering voices of the approaching men, but could not understand what they were saying. In his still-dazed condition Ki thought for an instant that he was in some delusion and imagining the sounds, for though he could see their feet strike, his ears picked up only the faintest whisper of the thuds that followed.

Ki suddenly realized that the shot which had grazed his head had robbed him of part of his hearing. He stayed pressed to the ground, straining to hear. Soon their voices began coming to him a bit louder, but while he could hear the voices, he could not make out the words. Then their voices stopped and after a few more thunks the sounds of their footsteps also ended. Ki slitted his eyelids. Without moving his head he could see nothing but three pairs of booted legs a yard or more away.

Although he was still balanced on the needlepoint between consciousness and insensibility, Ki realized that his only chance was to lie completely motionless and hope that the men approaching would think him dead and would not examine him too closely. He inhaled deeply and held his breath. Then one of the group spoke.

"You better see if he's still alive, Blade. And see if he's got anything on him that's worth taking."

Ki heard the scuff of booted feet approaching and hastily filled his lungs again. He was lying motionless once more before he felt rough hands dipping into the pockets of his loose jacket, and trying to find pockets in his trousers. The searcher discovered Ki's *ko-dachai* and slid the short blade from its leather sheath before rolling him over on his side, seeking a holstered gun. Then the man released him and stood up.

"He ain't packing iron, Mole," he said loudly. "All I got off him was a little knife, and it ain't such a much. He didn't have no pants pockets nor no money, neither."

"Damn it, Blade, is he dead or alive?"

"Dead as any other corpse I ever seen," Blade replied. His voice was fading and above it Ki could hear the man's footsteps retreating. Ki exhaled softly and breathed deeply but silently.

"I was right, Mole," the man said. His voice was farther from Ki's ears now. "Like I told you when he dropped, he's deader'n a doormat. He won't be snooping around no more."

"I figured I'd finished him," Mole replied. "It ain't often that I miss, and you know that for a fact, Grizz."

"Well, I wasn't trying to run down your shooting," Grizz protested. "But it might be you didn't do us no favor."

"Meaning just what?" Mole asked.

"Dead men can't talk," Grizz replied. "But you can always finish off a live one after you've pumped him dry."

"Hell's bells, Grizz! We didn't need to try and find out nothing from that dead chink!" Mole retorted. "He wasn't nothing but a flunky, come here with that dame them high-graders is trying to swindle."

"I'd give a pretty to know who she is, too," Grizz commented. "Stands to reason she's got money to burn, or they wouldn't've set her up as their mark."

"Grizz hit it square, if I take his meaning rightly," Blaze broke in quickly. "Might be we'd get more outa somebody that'd pay a ransom for her than we stand to make from all them salted diamonds we scratched out."

"Now, that idee come to my mind, too," Mole said. "But if that diamond-salting crew brung her here, she'd be too rich for us to mess around with. Hell, we wouldn't just have the law after us. We'd have the Pinkertons and everybody else."

"There ain't much the law could do if we taken her across the border into Mexico," Grizz suggested. "And I'd take my chances with the Pinkertons once we're outa their own backyard."

"Now that might be another story," Mole replied.

"We ain't pushed for time," Grizz went on. "All we been hanging around here for is to find out if we missed any of the pockets them high-graders salted."

Mole paid no attention; he was still following his own train of thought when he went on: "And we ain't too far from Mexico now. Once we get to Yuma, we're home free. And it ain't all that far to Yuma, now. A two-day ride if we don't have to push, less if we don't mind killing our horses."

"I say we oughta stay and try for the woman," Blade told his companions. "And maybe find out if we missed any of the places them diamond high-graders salted."

"It makes sense," Mole agreed. "Having a big grubstake to carry along ain't going to hurt us a bit."

"It'll be good to have enough so we won't need to pull any jobs south of the border, too," Blade put in. "I had them Rurales down there after me once, and I don't mind telling you, I lucked out getting away from 'em. They got a bad habit of not taking prisoners."

"But they ain't going to push in on a deal like we got in mind," Grizz pointed out. "Not if we cross their palms with a few of our little diamonds."

"It's all settled, then," Mole said. "We'll make sure we got all the diamonds that was salted. After that, all we got to do is grab the woman and hit out for the border."

"What about the chink?" Grizz asked. "We going to bury him, or just leave his body lay?"

"He sure as hell ain't going to bother us no more," Mole replied. "And I never was one for digging. Just let's leave him where he is."

"Well, him being there won't spook me," Blade said. "I'll sleep tonight as good as always."

"We might not be here tonight," Mole told him. "Let's get back to the fire and do some scheming. It's pennies to pigtails that dame's going to come looking for the chink, seeing he's her servant. And when she does, we better have a plan ready about what to do after we grab her."

Ki remained motionless until the ghostly sounds of their boots on the soil no longer reached his ears. For the first time he thought it was safe to rise to his feet.

He stood up, but even before he was fully erect a wave of giddiness swept over him. The smattering of anatomy that Ki had picked up in his busy and varied life was just enough to enable him to diagnose his problem. Until time took its effect on his injured ears and they returned to normal, he would be able to move only slowly and carefully; he would not be able to run without risking a fall.

Even that knowledge did not deter him. Though his mind was not functioning with its usual quick clarity, Ki knew what he must do. Slowly, moving inches at a time, he began to drag himself along the ground to get closer to the outlaws' campfire.

"It sure won't take us long to get to the other side of the sink," Tek Powell remarked as he pulled the saddle cinch tight on his horse's belly. "When you come right down to it, we don't even know that your man was anywhere near the place that shot came from."

"If you have any objections to going, I'm sure we can get along without you," Jessie said coldly. "In fact, if any of you don't care to go, I won't mind going alone."

"You know we wouldn't even think of letting you do that, Miss Starbuck," Benson said. "You're our guest here and we aim to take good care of you. Besides that, I've got a hunch we'll just run into a prospector who was shooting at a rabbit, or something like that."

Powell paid no attention to his companion's remark, but went on: "Even if we don't know for certain that your man Ki might be in trouble, we'd sure want to chase away any strangers—especially prospectors—that might be trying to jump our claim."

"It's odd you should call it your claim," Jessie said with a frown. "It was my understanding that you haven't filed a discovery claim here yet. And if you haven't, it's a matter of running a race to the nearest land office with anybody who might file one before you get around to doing it."

"Now, that's what we don't want to see happen," Benson broke in quickly, his eyes on Powell, his brows pulled together angrily. "Which is all the more reason for us going to take a look-see. Not that we ain't interested in helping your man at the same time, Miss Starbuck. If he's in trouble, we want to get him out of it just as fast as we can."

Belatedly, Powell said, "I hope you don't take what I just said wrong, Miss Starbuck. I'm sorry if I spoke outa turn, and I hope you'll let me apologize."

"Of course," Jessie said, nodding, her thoughts fixed less on her companions than on getting to the opposite side of the sink as quickly as possible. "Now, if we're ready, I suggest that we start without any more delay."

"Sure," Benson agreed. He turned to the others and went on: "We haven't got a lot of territory to cover, but we don't want to leave any holes for whoever's across the valley to slip through." Indicating Johnson, he went on: "Jack, you take the right-hand rim of the sink. Tek, you cut a shuck up the floor of the sink and ride—oh, a mile or so this side of Jack. Me and Miss Starbuck will do the same on the left-hand side."

While Benson was speaking, Jessie had been studying the terrain. There was little to look at inside the sink's perimeter except raw open ground. Around its edges but disappearing almost completely in its oval-shaped central expanse, an occasional clump of prickly pear sprawled their broad oval spine-studded leaves. Along the perimeter, where the scant rain runoff had no opportunity to puddle, the wired crook-branched cholla held sway. The cholla grew thickly in several spots along the ragged rim of the saucerlike depression.

Now Jessie turned to Benson and said, "Wouldn't it be better if you rode along the sink's floor, and let me go around the rim of the valley on the left side? That way you'll be closer to both your friends and me."

"That's what I was about to get around to, Miss Starbuck," he agreed without hesitation. "You just took the words out of my mouth, you might say."

She could not tell from Benson's reply whether the arrangement she'd proposed had occurred to him as it had to her, or whether he accepted it so unhesitatingly because it coincided with a plan he'd been forming himself.

"Suppose we get started, then," Jessie suggested. "We don't really have very far to ride, but the longer we delay, the more danger Ki may be in."

★

Chapter 14

Jessie did not look back for the first few minutes after she had wheeled her horse away from Benson and reined it toward the edge of the sink. Not until she'd ridden up the long slope and was turning to follow the long curve of the depression did she glance down and back to see how Benson and Johnson and Powell were distributing themselves.

As far as Jessie could tell, none of the three had moved more than a foot or two from the positions they'd held during the brief session when she'd been with them, while they were agreeing on the sketchy plan they would follow. From their gestures, waving arms, and pointing fingers, the three swindlers were having some sort of argument, but at that distance from them and with the muffled thunking of the hooves of her mount in her ears, she could hear nothing of what they were saying.

Nor was it easy for Jessie to distinguish between the three men. The sun was behind them now. Its bright rays turned them into silhouettes, dark featureless figures outlined against the dazzling glare reflected from the almost white soil that covered the bottom of the sink. Jessie turned away for a moment to glance at the terrain ahead and make sure she was not veering from the course she'd elected to follow. She reached the crest of the slope and reined her mount to head it along the wide sweeping curve of the sink's rim.

She glanced behind her once more, and for a moment was tempted to wheel her horse and ride back, to have another try at spurring Jackson and Powell and Benson into moving promptly. Then, even while she was still debating the wisdom of going back, still twisting in her saddle to watch them, the trio reined their mounts around, kicked them into a gallop at once, and started back in the direction of the cabin.

Jessie did not need anyone to interpret the meaning of their move for her. What had happened after she'd ridden away had become obvious to her quick mind during the brief glance she'd taken. Faced with the prospect of a fight to keep their cheating scheme from being exposed, well aware of the shaky ground on which they'd put themselves, the three would-be swindlers had obviously decided to abandon their plans and run for cover.

Although Jessie had no positive assurance that Ki was in trouble, she had no intention of abandoning her effort to find him. She knew quite well that Ki would have been back some time ago if he'd been free to make his own choice. There was only one explanation for his delayed return that came to her mind, and she discarded it at once. It was not a pleasant one to think of.

Setting her jaw and peering ahead at the long sweeping curve of the sink's rim, she toed her horse to a faster pace.

• • •

With a silent breath of relief Ki stirred after the outlaw called Blade had returned to join his cronies at their campfire. Closing his eyes in an effort to lessen the throbbing in his head, he wriggled his fingers slowly and found that he could control them without trouble. He glanced toward the outlaws. They were paying no attention to him, and Ki tried to sit up, but the dizzying spasm that accompanied the effort forced him to drop prone again at once.

After he'd been lying quietly for a few moments, Ki's giddiness diminished, but it did not leave him entirely. He glanced toward the outlaws. They were leaning close together and speaking in low voices. Ki strained his ears in an effort to overhear what they were now saying, but his head was still filled with a strange echoing resonance and he could hear only an occasional word.

However, when Ki saw where the outlaw trio had settled down, he knew at once that he must get closer to them. Pressing himself close to the earth, he began pushing himself forward with his toes, *ninja*-fashion. He stopped often, after gaining a foot or more, and glanced at the outlaws to make sure he was not being noticed, then propelled himself ahead another few inches.

As Ki advanced he took advantage of his pauses to slip two *shuriken* from the case which the searching outlaw had overlooked. He kept one of the throwing-blades in the fingers of each hand and used the butt of his palms to shift the angle of his inching approach to bring himself closer to the trio of renegades. He had no doubt that any of the three would put a slug into him without hesitation if they saw him moving.

“Now, let’s go over it again,” Mole was saying when Ki was close enough to pick up the lowered voices of the three outlaws. “We fan out around the sink so as one of us is bound to be close enough to wherever the diamond salters might be to get our shots in at close range. And just be damn sure neither one of you wings the woman. She ain’t worth a plugged nickle to us dead.”

“Me and Blade is both smart enough to know that, Mole,” Grizz said. “Just like we’re smart enough to be sure our guns got ca’tridges in the chamber when we pull trigger.”

“Then if you’re sure you’re ready, let’s go do it,” Mole told them. “Just be sure we get those three fellows, then we can go grab the woman.”

Ki pressed himself even closer to the earth when the outlaws stood up and struck out toward the rim of the sink. After overhearing their plan to kill the three diamond swindlers in cold blood, he was tempted to follow the trio, but when he got to his feet after they’d started on their mission of murder, his head began swimming and his usually keen vision blurred. Ki realized at once that to trail the renegades would be an act of folly.

Not only was he still unable to move with his customary speed and agility, but he owed the diamond swindlers nothing. His first and only allegiance was to Jessie. She was the next target of Mole and his unsavory companions, Ki told himself, and it was his duty to recover quickly in order to be in shape to keep her out of the hands of Mole and his followers.

Wriggling around to find a more comfortable position on the rocky ground, Ki returned the *shuriken* he’d been holding to their carrying case and began the job of recovering.

Feet planted firmly on the shifting ground, Ki went through the five preliminary steps of *ibuki*, the breathing exercises he'd learned in his first visit to a *do*. Performing the brief ritual twice refreshed him so much that he moved to the more advanced form of the ancient *ninja* exercise. By the time he'd completed the seventeen steps it involved, each more demanding than the last, Ki was almost back to his usual form.

He'd started on a second round of the *ibuki* when the distant crack of a rifle shot broke the silence. The shot came from the direction of the sink. Ki was listening to its reverberations ripple through the air when a second and almost at once a third shot reached his ears. The last two reports broke the air so close together that they almost sounded as one.

Ki heeded the shots as he'd heed any warning. He went at once to the spot where he'd been lying when the outlaws left and took out the two *shuriken* which he'd returned to their case earlier. He stretched out on the ground, taking the same helpless position of assumed unconsciousness he'd been in when they left. Then he settled himself to wait.

His wait was not a long one. Mole's voice sounded above the gritting footsteps. "I got to give you credit, Blade. You and Grizz sure delivered when the chips was down. Now that we got rid of them diamond swindlers, all we got to do is go down in the sink and grab the dame, and then wait for the money to come in to ransom her."

"That's what I figure," Blade replied. "And on top of the ransom money, we still got the diamonds to keep us going."

"Why, we're gonna live like great big nabobs down

there in Mexico, we'll be so rich!" Grizz put in. "When you figure to start, Mole?"

"Soon as we get down in the sink and round up the dame," Mole told him. "And that ain't going to take us long. We'll go on down there soon as we pick up our gear and stow it in our saddlebags."

"Let's shake our shanks, then," Blade said. "The quicker we get outa this damn dry hole, the better I'll like it."

Hearing the outlaws boasting of the murders they'd committed and being reminded of the plans they had for Jessie roused Ki to a degree of anger which he rarely experienced. He started to rise and launch the attack he'd planned, but stopped quickly and settled back when the thudding of hoofbeats on the dry soil reached his ears. He dropped prone again and waited.

Jessie had tried several times to spur her horse to a faster gait, but the animal had begun to turn skittish. She'd reached one of the watershed areas of the sink's sloping rim where Ki had been slowed by the same whim of nature that was now slowing her, the stretch where the thin crust had formed on the unstable sand. Though Jessie's horse balked and reared, she forced the animal ahead, following Ki's footprints across the treacherous ground.

While she was encouraged by spotting Ki's footprints, the slower progress forced on her was increasing Jessie's sense of urgency. Each time the animal put down a hoof and felt the crust break away, it reared and began bucking, making it necessary for her to look away from the terrain ahead. Despite Jessie's skill as a rider, the animal was strange to her, and she had no choice but to settle for a much slower advance than she'd have liked.

Jessie smelled the smoke-taint in the warm clean desert air long before she saw the almost-invisible thread of smoke. It was as much a shimmer of heat waves as it was smoke, and eyes less keen than Jessie's might have missed it completely. Between her and the smoke there were two large stands of cholla, and while the tops of the cactus showed only occasional patches of blue sky between their long dangling thorny shoots, the slanted bottoms of the plants were barren of any growth except the long spines that shot like oversized needles from the zigzag cylinders.

Stopping short, Jessie dismounted and weighted the reins of her horse with a stone while she walked slowly and silently up to the stand of cacti. She might have been looking through a dozen telescopes at once. Through the small widely scattered spaces of the cactus stalks she glimpsed bits and pieces of the terrain beyond, barren stone-studded patches of earth.

Suddenly Jessie's eyes adapted to the broken vista, and now she found that she could catch glimpses of motion as well as flashes of color which were not found in nature. Now she began to piece together the zigzag jigsaw puzzle. Once Jessie was able to recognize the gray of a flannel shirt and the dun khaki hue of breeches. As the man she could not see fully turned, she got a fleeting glance at the butt of a revolver above the dark shining brown of its hip-holster.

Before she'd taken another half-dozen slow short steps, she heard a man speaking and stopped at once. In the silence of the desert air Mole's voice sounded very loud.

". . . we won't have no trouble rounding up the dame. Likely she'll be scared skittish by all the shooting. She's likely hiding in that shanty down below right now."

Though Jessie had been sure she'd come to the end of her search, the outlaw's words confirmed it. She slid her Colt from its holster. The weapon was the one she favored of all the pistols she possessed, a special revolver given her by Alex, with a barrel and cylinder bored to take a .44 cartridge on its .38 caliber frame.

Colt ready in her hand, Jessie stepped ahead with greater confidence now and rounded the cactus clump. Mole was standing with his back to her, while Grizz and Blade faced her across the fire. A thin haze of rising heat waves from the dying campfire blurred the pair to Jessie's eyes, but by their surprised looks Mole understood at once that they'd seen something unexpected, and anything unexpected meant danger to the outlaw's mind.

Mole had his Colt in his hand, but Jessie's trigger finger was already tightening. Her revolver barked a second or less before Mole's forefinger closed. His gun's report was an echo of Jessie's shot, but Mole's body was already buckling from the impact of her Colt's slug and the bullet from the pistol he was lifting sent up a spurt of dust from the arid stretch of ground between them.

Jessie was swinging her Colt toward Grizz and Blade. Both men were at mid-draw. Jessie's eyes caught a glimpse of shining steel arcing through the air while she was still swinging her Colt to cover the pair. The arc of steel vanished as Ki's first *shuriken* sliced into Blade's throat, but a second flash of steel was already cutting the air. The shining gleam stopped when the second whirling *shuriken* launched by Ki cut deeply into the outlaw's shoulder and his extended arm started sagging.

Jessie had Grizz in the Colt's sights now, and she triggered off her shot. Grizz whirled in a half-turn as the bullet from the Colt smashed into his chest only a fraction of a second after Ki's blade had found its mark. The impact of the slug twirled the outlaw in a half-turn that became a fall. When Grizz hit the ground, he lay motionless, his Colt still in his hand.

After the spurts of gunfire the silence of the sink's rim seemed intensified. The stillness lasted for only a moment, then Jessie called, "Ki? Are you all right?"

"As right as I'll ever be, Jessie," he replied, rising from his knees.

"Who are—I guess I'd better say who were these men, Ki?"

"Outlaws. I heard enough to know that after they captured me."

For the first time Jessie saw the dried blood on Ki's head and face. She exclaimed, "Ki! You're hurt!"

"It only hurts a little bit now. I was lucky."

"Did one of the outlaws shoot you?"

Though the admission ruffled his hurt pride, Ki would not lie to Jessie. He nodded and admitted, "Yes. But that was quite a while ago, Jessie. I'm afraid I was careless."

"But I heard shooting on the way here."

Ki gestured toward the bodies of the outlaws. "That was when they got the diamond swindlers."

"And what happened to the diamonds?" she asked.

"Some of them will probably turn up when we search these outlaws' saddlebags. And the swindlers may still have a few. But I'm sure we both know by now that there won't be any diamonds taken out of the ground."

Ki was surprised at the sudden smile that appeared in Jessie's face. She said, "I don't need any more diamonds, Ki. I've got a couple of diamond rings and a bracelet in the safe at the Circle Star, and that's where I intend to leave them. Now, if you're sure you feel all right, let's start back home."

Watch for

LONE STAR AND THE TEXAS KILLERS

eighty-sixth novel in the exciting
LONE STAR
series from Jove

coming in October!